NEVER TO BE TOLD

1967: Upon her death, Lucie Curtis's mother leaves behind a letter that sends her reeling — she was adopted when only a few days old. Soon Lucie is on her way to France to find the mother who gave birth to her during the war. But how can you find a woman who doesn't want to be found? And where does Lucie's adoptive cousin, investigative journalist Yannick, fit in? She is in danger of falling in love with him. However, does he want to help or hinder her in her search?

KATE FINNEMORE

◆

NEVER TO BE TOLD

Complete and Unabridged

LINFORD
Leicester

First published in Great Britain in 2018

First Linford Edition
published 2020

A catalogue record for this book is available
from the British Library.

ISBN 978–1–4448–4581–5

Published by
Ulverscroft Limited
Anstey, Leicestershire

Set by Words & Graphics Ltd.
Anstey, Leicestershire
Printed and bound in Great Britain by
T. J. International Ltd., Padstow, Cornwall

This book is printed on acid-free paper

Cruel Discovery

The jaunty notes of 'Penny Lane', the latest Beatles hit, pierced the quiet of the funeral. Lucie looked up as a young lad holding a boxy transistor radio to his ear sauntered past the cemetery wall.

Well, he wasn't to know, she thought. She stood by her mother's graveside, leaning against the solid strength of her stepfather's body, both her arms wrapped round one of his.

Her mother's sister Arlette stood on his other side, her pillbox hat with its veil pulled down over her face, bringing a touch of French chic to a very English gathering.

Arlette's son Yannick had put his arm round his mother, drawing her to him. It had been touch and go whether he'd have recovered enough to leave hospital and cross the Channel.

1

Lucie was glad for his sake he'd been able to make it in time.

She squeezed her stepfather's arm, the reassurance for herself as much as for him. The cancer had taken her beloved mother with cruel speed. Now she was gone and Lucie felt an unbearable sense of loss. Her stepfather did, too, she knew.

He stood there, stock still, his already pale face washed of colour, a bewildered flickering of the eyes his only movement.

He'd adored his wife with a deep, protective passion ever since the day he'd met her in France almost 20 years before, a penniless widow with her five-year-old daughter Lucie, in those bleak years after the war.

'Earth to earth. Ashes to ashes. Dust to dust.'

As if at some unspoken signal, the other mourners — there must have been more than 50 of them — moved forward, murmuring quiet words to Lucie, her stepfather, her aunt, her cousin, patting their arms, gripping their shoulders, dropping bright tokens of farewell into the grave.

Tears filled Lucie's eyes, and a lump, achingly painful, bitter with the unfairness of it all, rose in her throat. Fifty-five. It was no age at all. Far too young to die.

'Lucie.' Her stepfather took her hands in both his. Apart from Arlette and her son, who stood murmuring quietly to each other a few yards away, the two of them were alone.

'When we get home, when everyone's gone . . . ' he took a deep breath as though steeling himself, 'I've got to talk to you. It's something very important.'

The urgency of his tone was like a shock of iced water. Him, too? Fate couldn't be so callous. Could it?

'Tell me now.'

Ray Curtis shook his head.

'Later.' He urged her towards her aunt and cousin. 'I'm sorry,' he added. 'I shouldn't have brought it up. It's, uh, been preying on my mind.'

Lucie fell in beside Yannick, and Ray beside Arlette, as they followed the other mourners past the knapped-flint cottages to the Old Rectory.

'I'm sorry I couldn't get to see Margot,' Yannick said to her in his faultless English, 'before she . . .'

With an effort, Lucie pushed her stepfather's words out of her mind.

'She understood. Believe me, she understood. She knew you were busy having bits of bullet dug out of you.'

'One of the joys of being a war correspondent. The doctors tell me I can go back to work,' he added, 'but I've got to take it easy for the next six months. I'm not sure I'll be going back there. Certainly not in the immediate future.'

'Won't you miss it?'

'Maybe it's time to try something else,' he said after a brief pause.

The years in Vietnam, and the injury that had brought him back to France — both had left their mark, Lucie thought. He walked with a slight limp

4

— that would disappear, though, she imagined.

But there was a lean strength about him now in the lines of his face and in the way he walked that hadn't been there before. Mental toughness too, she sensed, in the way he approached the world.

The next hour, two hours — Lucie had no idea how long — went by in a blur. At the Old Rectory, along with several others, she passed round cucumber sandwiches, offered cups of tea and talked about her mother.

Sharing her grief brought a strange kind of comfort. She listened with a soft, absent smile to her mother's friends' and neighbours' stories.

Often, her mind was elsewhere, back in the past, while her eyes went constantly to her stepfather. How was he faring? And what was it he had to tell her?

He stood by the fire. He wasn't alone, there was always someone with him, but his gaze returned time after time to the photo on the mantelpiece of himself, his wife, and Lucie.

At last all the guests had gone.

'I'll clear all this away,' Arlette said, speaking in French as she normally did. 'Help me, please, Yannick.'

'We'll go into my study, Lucie.' Her stepfather held the door open for her. 'Good to see Yannick, eh?'

He was making small talk, delaying the moment, Lucie thought, looking at him with anxious eyes.

'Yes, it is. Tell me . . . '

'Sit down, Lucie, please.' He gestured to the swivel chair by the desk before pacing over to the window. He gazed out across the garden but Lucie was sure he wasn't seeing a thing.

'Dad, tell me what it is.'

'It's . . . um . . . ' He came over to the desk, close to her, picked up a pile of exercise books waiting to be marked, then set them down again.

He picked up his pipe, seemed to think better of it, and put it down on the desk. Lucie's stomach churned.

She'd never seen him so irresolute.

He cleared his throat and began again.

'Your mother . . . um . . . ' He perched on the edge of the desk, taking both her hands in his. 'Your mother left two letters. One for you, one for me. To be opened only after her death. I read my one this morning.'

'Yes?' she prompted when he fell silent.

In the end the words came in a rush.

'There's no easy way to tell you this, Lucie. She's not your mother, it turns out. She adopted you when you were only a few days old.'

For long seconds Lucie just looked at him, too stunned to speak. His words simply made no sense. She shook her head, as if the action could wish them away, back into his mouth.

'Adopted me? I don't understand.'

'Let me finish. There's more.' His grip on her fingers tightened. 'You were . . . the French say '*née sous X*'.'

Lucie stared at him. She wanted to

back away, all her senses recoiling already from what it was he had to tell her.

Her mouth was dry. She ran her tongue across her lips.

'I know what the words say. 'Born under X'.' Her voice faltered, sharp with anxiety. 'But what does it mean?'

A Comforting Presence

''Born under X'.' Lucie turned to look at Yannick. He'd suggested a walk, and they were now taking the path to the beach that they'd taken during countless childhood summers.

'Well, you work for a French newspaper. You must have heard of it. You must know what it means. My mother, whoever she is, didn't put her name on my — well, the French equivalent of a birth certificate. She just put an X. The letter X.'

There was bewilderment in Lucie's voice, and pain. She dug her hands into the pockets of her long black coat. The fingers of her left hand touched the envelope containing her mother's — no, not her mother's! — letter. She would read it, but not yet.

She heard Yannick's swift intake of breath, saw his slight stumble when they emerged from the path on to the beach.

'Will you be OK? Your leg — going over the stones?' The keen April wind whipped strands of her hair round her face.

'I'm fine. Really.'

But she saw him wince as a pebble moved under his foot.

'Here, take my hand,' she said.

His strong warm fingers curled round hers and they scrunched across the shingle, heading for the water's edge.

She liked the feel of his hand round hers. They'd held hands as children, she remembered, had stopped doing so as self-conscious teenagers.

'She wanted to stay anonymous,' she said, returning to the subject that was uppermost in her mind. 'Totally anonymous. She gave birth to me anonymously. There's no way of knowing who she was.

'Who she is,' she amended. 'Chances are she's still alive.' She stopped, conscious of sounding like a needle stuck in the same groove of a record.

The two of them had reached the steep bank that marked the high-tide point, and Lucie paused, breathing in the tang of the seaweed and the salt-laden air.

In the fading light, the grey of the sea merged with the grey of the sky. The waves crashed on the shingle, dragging over it as the sea pulled back out. Seagulls wheeled and screeched in the air overhead.

Letting go of Yannick's hand, she tucked her hair behind her ears. He was a good listener, she decided. He'd listened — intently, she sensed. Yes, he'd thrown in a question here and there, but he hadn't tried to stop her, or interrupted, or argued with her, and it occurred to her that he knew she'd needed to rant, to get the anguish and pain out of her system.

She took a step forward, and slipped, nearly losing her balance. Pebbles skittered, clattering down and she slid with them. It could almost be a metaphor for what her life had suddenly become, she thought. All the old certainties had shifted beneath her feet.

The woman she'd considered all her life to be her mother wasn't her mother. Arlette, Margot's sister, wasn't her aunt. Yannick wasn't her cousin.

And the barely remembered man in a white chemist's coat smelling of carbolic soap wasn't her birth father, she realised with a shock. Lucie no longer knew who she was.

Oh, but she did, she thought with a twist of bitter anger, moving across to the water's edge. She was the child of a woman who'd wanted rid of her as soon as she was born. The child of a woman who couldn't even bring herself to give her new-born baby her surname.

'Now I know why I looked nothing like my mother.' She spoke as much to herself as to Yannick.

He stood behind her, had placed his hands on her upper arms, a comforting presence.

It was impossible to hide the notes of fresh hurt and bewilderment in her voice. She was tall and long-boned. She'd been the tallest in her class at school, and taller than most of her fellow students at RADA.

Copper glinted in her hair, her eyes were green with hazel flecks, and the skin of her face was fair and dusted with freckles.

Surprisingly, perhaps, in view of her nationality, she looked very English, unlike her mother who'd always been so very French with her petite build, neat dark hair, brown eyes and complexion that tanned easily.

'I always assumed I took after my father.' She pulled away. Looking down, she kicked at a stone. 'But obviously I don't. Not the man I thought was my father, at least.'

She stooped, picked the stone up, and hurled it out to sea.

'Such a cruel, heartless law.' Tears had filled her eyes. 'What were the stupid French thinking of when . . . '

Abruptly she turned, and he took her in his arms, drawing her head down on to his shoulder.

'Stupid French? Don't forget you're French, too. The only reason you're here in England is because your mother — your adoptive mother — was widowed and married an Englishman.'

His tone was mild, but it was a rebuke nonetheless and Lucie felt colour spread across her cheeks.

'I'm sorry. You're right.' Her voice was muffled against the fabric of his coat. He smelt of a lemony aftershave lotion.

'You've got to remember . . .'

'What?' She lifted her head from his shoulder.

He shook his head.

'No, forget it.'

'Tell me,' she insisted. 'You can't leave it like that.'

The briefest of pauses. Then he spoke.

'You've got to remember you're seeing things through nineteen-sixties

14

eyes. But the war had only just finished in France when you were born. Things were different then.'

What he said made sense. But as they turned and headed back to the Old Rectory, walking side by side, Lucie couldn't rid herself of the conviction he'd been about to say something else entirely.

Something he'd decided she wouldn't want to hear.

An Uncertain World

Lucie's stepfather and aunt were in the sitting-room, side by side on the two-seater sofa by the fire, the photograph album open on their laps. Both looked up, concern in their eyes, as Lucie came into the room.

Lucy gave a nod and a glimmer of a smile to reassure them, pulled off her coat and tossed it over the chair by the door.

The skirt of her dress, a 1920s black crepe she'd bought for a shilling at a jumble sale, swayed as she crossed the room. There were questions she wanted to ask her aunt.

But Arlette forestalled her, standing up and patting her arm.

'I must see to supper,' she said, heading for the kitchen. Like her sister, she loved cooking, and loved showing the English how food should be cooked.

Lucie sat down on the sofa next to her stepfather. He set his pipe down, pushed the photograph album to one side and put his arm round her.

'Where's Yannick?'

'In your study. He's got some phone calls to make.'

'Read your mother's letter yet?'

'No.' She sucked in a long breath. 'Can I still think of her as my mother? Why didn't she tell me before? I don't know who I am any more.'

And all at once the tears were there, a blessed release as she buried her face against her stepfather's shoulder, letting her pain and bewilderment flow.

He hugged her tight and made soothing noises. They were in the same boat, she thought. Both had lost someone very dear to them, and the bombshell that person had dropped had affected — and would affect — both their lives.

Long minutes later, when the crying had lessened, Lucie pulled away and sat up.

'Thanks, Dad.' Her voice was shaky still.

'Why don't you look at the photos with me?' her stepfather said, sliding the album on to their laps.

'It's not too painful, all those memories?' She brushed away the last of the tears with the heel of her hand.

'No.' But his eyes were over-bright. 'Strangely enough, it helps. It's a comfort.'

Giving his hand a reassuring squeeze, she looked down at the photograph album. It was open at one of the early pages and showed a five-year-old Lucie at a zoo in France, ribbons in her hair, a solemn expression on her face as she tugged at her mother's hand, clearly too impatient to wait for the photo to be taken. Ray was looking on fondly.

'You were a determined little thing, even at that age. You wanted to see the giraffes and you certainly didn't want to wait for the photographer to take the photo.'

Lucie slowly turned the pages, looking at the faded black and white photos, a smile on her face and in her heart.

Her father was right, it was a comfort. Her world had shifted, turned upside down. She was still in shock. She needed the reassurance of the past she knew.

'Tell me how you met my mother,' she invited. *My mother*. She couldn't think of her in any other way.

'You must be sick and tired of that old story by now.'

Lucie shook her head.

'I'll start it for you. At the end of the war you were demobbed, you went to university to study French and German, and after that you spent a year in the French city of Poitiers teaching English while perfecting your French. Your turn.'

'Well, it was fairly soon after I'd arrived in Poitiers.' Her stepfather picked up his pipe and tobacco pouch from the small table at his side. As he spoke, he teased out the long strands of tobacco before tamping them down into the bowl of his pipe. 'My landlady's son had lent me his moped. The cobbles were uneven and slippery with rain, and I was wobbling along when a delivery van reversed into me. I must have been knocked unconscious for a second or two.

'Next thing I knew, I opened my eyes to find I was lying on the cold ground surrounded by a group of people speaking nineteen to the dozen in a patois I didn't understand.

'One of them,' his voice slowed, had a gruffness to it now, 'Margot, of course, stood out from the crowd. She kneeled down beside me and wiped the rain and mud from my face with her handkerchief.' He smiled.

'It smelled of lavender. She got a couple of the men to carry me into the chemist's where she worked. It was only a few metres away.' He put the pipe in his mouth and brought his lighter to the bowl.

'And that was it,' he said, puffing at the pipe to get it going. 'I was hooked. It was love at first sight.'

Sitting in the warmth of the fire, close to the man she'd always thought of as her father, Lucie was moved more than ever that day by his story.

She looked at the photo of the chemist's shop. It stood on the corner where two cobbled streets met, part of a row of shops. Wearing a long white coat and smiling radiantly, Margot stood outside it on the narrow pavement that sloped uphill behind her, holding Lucie by the hand.

Her stepfather traced his fingertips across the surface of the photo, softly circling his wife's face. He sighed.

'Your mother never gave any hint that you were not her child,' he said. There was sadness in his voice, and Lucie thought how much it must hurt that the wife he'd adored had kept something from him. 'We never managed to give you a little brother or sister but I rather assumed that was down to me.'

'It doesn't matter.' Although it had. When she was at school, being an only child had been yet another thing that had set her apart from her classmates.

'Lucie, you're still my daughter, stepdaughter, adopted daughter — call it what you will. As far as I'm

21

concerned you've been my daughter for almost twenty years, and you'll always be my daughter.'

She reached across and squeezed her stepfather's hand.

'I know. Thank you,' she said, grateful for this one certainty in a now uncertain world.

A lump of coal stirred on the fire. Delicious smells wafted from the kitchen. Onion, bacon. And garlic. Where on earth had Arlette found that? It was warm and cosy sitting beside her stepfather and for a while Lucie found a kind of peace after the shocks of the afternoon.

He flicked over the pages of the album, stopping when he came to a double-page spread of photos, recent ones in colour, showing Lucie in four roles she'd played, two on stage and two on television.

There was the Lady Macbeth she'd played in modern dress, the 'Wednesday Play' role of a young woman battling in vain against the stigma of being an unmarried mother, her second television part as the wife of a rapist in 'Z-Cars', and the role of Joan of Arc in Anouilh's 'L'Alouette' for a company that had toured France the summer before.

Very different roles, but what all four had in common was that she always played strong women. Her height was a factor, of course, as was the bone structure of her face. Only her eyes, a fragile green in certain lights, seemed to contradict the strength of her other features.

'You know your mother was extremely proud of you. And so am I.'

'I still spend most of my time working in pubs to make ends meet,' Lucie said ruefully.

It had been three years since she'd graduated from RADA and her career was hardly a roaring success. She had yet to make the big breakthrough. Her agent was working on it though, and recently she'd been for three auditions, one for Granada, the commercial television company, and the others for the BBC.

Arlette's voice, calling from the

dining room, broke the short, comfortable silence.

'Supper's ready.'

'Arlette,' Lucie said when the four of them were sitting round the dining table, 'did you have any idea I was adopted?'

Arlette put her knife and fork down.

'I've been thinking about that, and the answer is no, I didn't. It was wartime, remember, and I didn't see Margot for years.'

Lucie glanced across at Yannick, sitting opposite her. He, too, was listening intently.

'Back in 1942,' Arlette continued, 'the Germans — well, the French government, too — wanted people to go and work in Germany. It was a kind of moral blackmail, really. For every three people who volunteered, one French prisoner of war would be freed.

'And by then they'd been prisoners for over two years. So your uncle Charles and I, we volunteered. As we saw it, we were doing our patriotic duty,

24

helping our soldiers see their families again.'

'A scheme put forward by a collaborationist government,' Yannick cut in. His tone was scathing. 'A scheme doomed to failure.'

'There was no way of knowing that at the time,' his mother shot back. Her voice softened as she went on. 'And what we also didn't know at the time, Yannick, was that I was expecting you. Luckily the Germans gave me a job in a children's home and I was able to keep you with me.'

She looked at Lucie, shaking her head.

'When we got back to France, at the end of Forty-four, Margot had had you. Or so I thought. I never thought to question it. I knew she and Fernand had been trying for a baby for years and I was so pleased they'd finally managed it.

'You were three months old, masses of fine dark hair on your head and a lovely smile, such a sweet little thing.'

There was a moment of silence.

'So no-one ever knew,' Lucie said at last.

'Fernand . . . her husband . . . your — ' Arlette broke off. 'I was going to say 'your father', but he wasn't your father, was he? He must have known, but he never said anything. Not to me at least.'

So Many Questions

Later that evening, in the privacy of her room, Lucie was finally calm enough to open the letter her mother — no, not her mother — had written for her.

She got into bed, pulling the blankets and eiderdown up to her chin, conscious of a churning apprehension in her stomach. Just like the minutes before she went on stage.

She paused, one part of her fully aware that she was putting the fateful moment off. Her mouth was dry as she turned the envelope over and over in her hands.

She was scared. She was hoping for something from this letter, hoping to discover some answers. The risk of disappointment, of not finding those answers, was almost more than she could bear.

The envelope was surprisingly bulky.

Lifting the flap, Lucie drew out two sheets of the stiff, quality notepaper Margot always used, and another envelope. It was sealed, and had no address on it, just the name 'Mélusine' in her mother's handwriting.

Lucie put it to one side and turned her attention to the notepaper, surprised to see several crossings-out. So unlike her mother, normally so neat and precise in everything she did.

2nd April 1967

My dearest darling daughter,

This is the hardest letter I've ever had to write. How can I even begin to explain why I never told you that you were adopted? I should have told you, I know. I feel consumed by guilt.

I've tried to tell you several times in the last weeks, each time you came down from London, but something stopped me every time, I don't know what.

Lying here in bed I've been thinking about it, what happened all those years ago. There was no point in telling you when you were little, obviously, as you just wouldn't have understood. Then Ray came along and I just couldn't bring myself to tell him — how would he have reacted to knowing you were not my husband's child?

I could never give you up, that goes without saying, but I was frightened of losing him, too, the most wonderful man in the world. I couldn't risk it so I stayed silent. So there were two of you to tell, and it just got harder and harder the longer I left it. How could I ever explain why I'd left it so long? And you both know now that I left it to the very end. I took the coward's way out, writing this letter and the one for Ray. I'm so, so sorry for that.

When we first came to England, you and I, with Ray, the kids in your class laughed at you, do you remember, because you had three Christian names? I've told you this story before

29

— well, no, I've told you a version of this story that glossed over the truth — so I'll tell you the full story now.

I chose your third name, Dieudonnée — gift of God — because that's exactly what you were, a gift from God, a miracle, the baby I never thought I'd have.

Fernand and I had been trying for a baby for ages but nothing happened. A doctor friend of ours said he knew someone who was having a baby but couldn't keep it and had to give it up for adoption — did we want it? Well, of course we said yes, and our doctor friend brought you along to us a couple of months later.

I'm crying as I write this, remembering how happy Fernand and I were to be holding you in our arms. It was overwhelming, the most beautiful experience of our lives together.

What I didn't tell you before was that it wasn't me but your birth mother who chose your other names. I don't know why. I never had any contact with her, so couldn't ask her. We were just told we had to call you Mélusine Jeanne, so it must have been important to her.

I think another reason I didn't tell you you were adopted, especially in the early years — or am I just trying to justify the unjustifiable? — is that you already had so much to cope with.

Schoolchildren can be so cruel. When we came to England you didn't speak any English, obviously, and your classmates laughed at you, then when you'd picked up quite a bit of English they laughed at your French accent.

Whatever you did, you couldn't win, and I know you often felt an outsider here in England. I know the name Mélusine caused you problems, too — you made the right choice to change it.

I hope you can find it in your heart to forgive me. What I did, or rather, what I didn't do, was unforgivable. I was a coward, couldn't bring myself to say something which might have shattered the happiness the three of us had found together. And as I said, the longer I left it, the harder it got.

I'm thinking of the future now. I'm near the end of my life and I won't be around much longer to help and support you. Not that you need my help and support much any more. You are a strong, courageous young woman.

You've chosen a difficult profession but I know you've got the guts and determination to make a go of it. I wish I was going to live long enough to see it happen, but I'm rather afraid it isn't to be.

Look after your stepfather and remember he loves you and has always loved you as if you were his own child. As have I.

The letter ended at that point. There was no signature. No stock formula for ending a letter. Neither was necessary. Her mother's voice spoke to her through every word, as if she were in the room beside her, hugging her close.

Tears spilled down Lucie's cheeks. She tried to hold them back but it was no use.

Her mother's love had been unconditional. She had loved her, had supported and protected her throughout her childhood and on into adulthood.

Lucie had been so lucky. And now she'd lost her to a pitiless disease. Never again would she experience the depth of her mother's love for her.

With a shudder Lucie recalled the problem with her name that her mother had hinted at in her letter. It was the October after her sixth birthday. She'd been barely a month in her new school in England. Finding the name Mélusine both weird and exotic, her classmates had shortened it to Melly. But Carol Banfield the class bully — Lucie remembered the name to this day — had yelled out, 'Smelly Melly!', picked up immediately by the others making 'oink' noises and shouting 'Pooh!'

Lucie had punched the bully in the stomach before running off the school field, crying as she'd never cried before, somehow finding her way the two miles back to home.

Her mother had been there to hold her in her arms and wipe her face dry, fighting back her anger and the distress she felt for her daughter, but it was Lucie herself who had concocted her new name using the middle syllables of the name Mélusine.

Picking the other envelope up, she opened it with shaking fingers and took out two sheets of paper, each folded in four.

As she unfolded the first one, she saw the title *ACTE DE NAISSANCE*: her birth certificate. Eagerly she read it through, a single long paragraph written in a careful longhand, the black ink already rusting with age.

Following the ruling of the Court dated the tenth of November nineteen hundred and forty-four let it be known that Mélusine Jeanne Dieudonnée Bondel was born on the twenty-ninth of July nineteen forty-four at eleven in the evening at 2 impasse de la Gare, Poitiers, Vienne, a girl, daughter of Fernand Michel Bondel, pharmacist, living at 25 rue de la Sainte-Marie, Poitiers, Vienne, born in Poitiers in 1903 and of Margot Elisabeth Monier, his wife, no profession, living at the same address, born in Poitiers in 1912.

There followed the registrar's signature and official stamp. Lucie stared at the sheet of paper, frowning, both puzzled and disappointed. Was that it?

She wasn't sure what she'd been expecting, but if she'd been hoping for some amazing revelation it hadn't been forthcoming.

The document told her almost nothing that was new: the exact address where she'd been born, that was all. It didn't say Margot and Fernand had adopted her. And there was no mention at all of her birth mother, not even an

'X' where her name might have been.

Frowning still, Lucie unfolded the second sheet of paper, typewritten this time. She read the first few lines and her heart stood still for an instant.

Ruling pronouncing the adoption of Mélusine Jeanne France (Mélusine Jeanne Dieudonnée Bondel) . . .

Was it possible? She scanned the rest of the page. Yes! She could have shouted for joy.

Someone in the Court offices must have made a mistake. Her former surname was surely her mother's surname too. Her mother was no longer anonymous. She had a surname at least.

No. Lucie leaned back against the headboard, thoughts swirling uneasily. Something was wrong. It was too easy. French bureaucrats didn't make mistakes like that. There was something here she didn't understand.

Still, she had an address. It was a start.

Uneasy Suspicions

When she went downstairs the next morning, Lucie could hear the murmur of Yannick and Arlette's voices, the clatter of pans and the chink of crockery from the kitchen.

Her stepfather was in the lounge, playing the gentle, lilting melody of Trenet's 'La Mer' on the piano. He was wearing his tweed jacket with the leather elbow patches, ready for a day's work. He was head of modern languages at the local boys' grammar school.

'One of her favourites,' Lucie murmured, standing beside him.

'She loved it here by the sea.' He slid along the piano stool and Lucie sat down beside him.

'She'd been afraid you wouldn't want her, you'd dump her if you knew I wasn't her child,' Lucie said.

'Never.' He stopped playing and

turned to face her. 'I'd never have done that. I'd fallen in love with both of you. But I can understand why she was scared. Things were desperate for her in those years after the war.

'Fernand had been killed in a car crash, she had you but no money coming in apart from what she could earn. And women couldn't earn much in those days, believe you me. Not that it's much better now.

'She had two rooms over what had been her shop, hers and Fernand's. She'd had to sell to pay off his debts. The new owner let her continue working there.

'But I remember how cold it was that winter. She had a one-bar electric fire but couldn't afford to have it on much — no money to pay the electricity. And the two of you were stick-thin.' He frowned.

'Don't think, though, that she just saw me as some kind of saviour, a way out for her, a meal-ticket. It wasn't like that at all. She fell in love with me just as much as I fell for her.' His eyes clouded, his fingers tracing random notes on the piano. 'I'm going to miss her so much.'

Lucie's thoughts went to her mother's letter, and the depth of the love she'd poured out to her daughter.

'Me too,' she added quietly.

She stood up and moved over to the mantelpiece, smoothing her fingers over the curves of the gilded bronze clock her mother had snapped up at a bargain price in a local antiques shop.

Her stepfather was playing another Trenet song but she scarcely heard it. Scarcely heard, either, the click as the kitchen door opened and Yannick or Arlette, or both, came into the room.

Her mind was elsewhere. She'd slept badly, thoughts, memories, feelings circling in an endless round in her brain. In those long, dark, sleepless hours she'd come to a decision.

She drew in a long breath.

'I need to find out about my birth mother. Who she is. Why she couldn't put her name to my birth. Why she couldn't acknowledge me.'

Hurt and bewilderment welled up, just as they had when she'd first found out. She turned back to her stepfather, and was surprised to see Yannick leaning back against the kitchen door.

'I didn't hear you come in.'

He pushed himself away from the door.

'You were born 'under X'. You won't find your birth mother. Ever. It's impossible.'

His tone was neutral, as was the expression on his face. But the way he thrust his hands into the pockets of his trousers as he came towards her, favouring his injured leg, told a different story. Lucie sensed he was holding himself in check. As though he were trying not to cause her pain.

Her chin came up.

'You can't know that.'

'You've lived most of your life in England. I've lived in France, and I've heard the stories, read about the heartbreak. I'll say again — finding her will be impossible.'

'I've got an address. Maybe a name, too.'

'Impossible.'

Her stepfather still sat on the piano stool, hands resting lightly on the keys. She could see concern in his eyes. In Yannick's, too, she thought.

An uneasy knot twisted deep in her stomach, that same unease she'd felt on the beach when Yannick had started to say something, had changed his mind.

'You're a journalist. If you know something you think I . . . '

'I know no more than you.' He turned away, pushing long fingers through his thick dark hair. 'But think through all the implications before you do anything rash.' He turned back to face her. 'Promise me that, at least.'

For a long moment, shaken, she simply met his gaze. He raised a questioning eyebrow and she swallowed, tried to smile, make light of it.

'I promise.'

41

A Dream Come True

'Which do you want first, the good news or the bad news?' Her agent's voice, as bright and enthusiastic as ever, reverberated down the phone line.

Lucie laughed.

'How can you be so relentlessly cheerful so early in the morning, Helena?' She glanced at her wristwatch. Nine-thirty. Not so early.

With one hand she tugged the collar of her dressing gown up around her ears. Even though it was near the end of May, the narrow hallway outside her bedsit, with its draughts and lino floor, was chilly.

'Well?'

'Bad news first.' Lucie's eye was caught by the envelope on top of the untidy heap of letters on the hall table. Someone from one of the other bedsits must have picked it up and put it there.

The crossed flags franked along the top edge were red, white and blue. Her heart gave a little leap. A letter from one of the town halls in France she'd written to.

She twisted it round, trying to read the postmark. Merton-les-Bois. A small town not far from Poitiers, she recalled. Maybe this time . . .

With a start she realised she hadn't been listening.

'Sorry. Could you say that again, please?'

A hint of exasperation entered the agent's voice.

'OK. They don't want you for 'Z-Cars'. Your features are too distinctive, they say. People will remember you from when you played Irene.'

Lucie's attention switched abruptly from the letter to the phone call. It could only mean one thing.

'And the good news?' She didn't dare hope.

'The new soap!' Lucie could almost hear the exclamation mark. 'You've got the part of Dr Jamieson's girlfriend! Rehearsals start end of August. Congratulations!'

Lucie's world stood still for an instant. Then her thoughts began darting in all directions. Questions spilled out. A broad, joyful smile lit her face. Some five minutes later when she put the phone down she practically danced back into her bedsit.

She hadn't absorbed half the information Helena had given her, she was sure, but it didn't matter. Her agent would put it all in writing. She was light-headed with happiness. It was amazing news. A dream come true. This could be her big break.

She swivelled on her heels, turning back to the door. She had to ring her stepfather, share her good fortune with him. He'd be so pleased for her.

At the door, though, she paused. Her mother — adoptive mother — wasn't there to hear her news, of course. It was just over a month since she'd died, and Lucie's sense of loss remained a raw wound that wouldn't heal.

No, she wouldn't tell her stepfather yet. Besides, the prospect of regular work must not be allowed to alter the frugal habits of the last few years. She'd phone that evening when the cheap rate operated.

Blankly, she looked at the envelope she held in her hand, remembered, and tore it open. It was typewritten and in French, short and to the point.

We regret to inform you that we do not disclose by post information of the type you request.

It was brutally concise. Bitterly, she observed that the formula which merely ended the letter, Dickensian in its floweriness, was longer than the main body of the letter.

Lucie sank down into the armchair by the window, tucking her long legs up beneath her. She needed to think things through.

An idea had been circling in her mind ever since she'd first found out about the circumstances of her birth, and the morning's news helped give it concrete shape. It was time to take stock.

Margot would always be the woman who had brought her up, who had loved her as only a mother could.

But at the same time she wasn't her mother, and it had somehow become important to Lucie to find out who her real mother was, and why she'd needed to abandon her daughter.

The day after the funeral she'd spoken with her aunt. Try as she might, she couldn't think of Margot, Arlette, or Yannick, as anything other than her mother, aunt, or cousin.

'I don't give much for your chances,' Arlette had said, her voice heavy with pessimism. 'There are ads in the papers all the time from people desperate to trace their birth mothers. It's heart-breaking, it really is. Every now and again, very rarely, there's a story about someone who's found their mother, but it's a fluke, pure chance.'

'I've got a name and an address, remember,' Lucie said.

Her aunt sent her a long look and shook her head.

'I think Yannick was right. It's not going to be as easy as you imagine.'

It had been a flying visit for her son. He'd arrived the morning of the funeral and had left 24 hours later. The editor of the 'Clairon Hebdomadaire', the much-respected weekly magazine Yannick worked for, had wanted him back. The house seemed strangely empty without him, Lucie thought.

The school in Tours where Arlette taught history and geography had given her generous time off for her sister's funeral, and she wouldn't be leaving till the weekend.

'People aren't given an actual birth certificate like in England,' she went on. 'The records are kept at the town hall of the town where you're born. If you need a certificate for some reason, you go along and ask for a copy. That's what Margot must have done. So, Poitiers town hall, that's who you need to contact.' She looked across at her niece, concern shadowing her face. 'They might be able to help you. But I doubt it.'

'There's always the possibility,' her stepfather added, 'if your birth mother wanted to remain anonymous that she arranged for the birth to be registered in another town.'

'I'm not sure she could do that,' Arlette said. 'But, as I say, it'll be pure chance if you do find her.'

Despite their lack of encouragement Lucie's natural optimism had come to the fore and, back in her bedsit in London, she'd sat down with high hopes to compose her letter to the town hall in Poitiers.

'I would be grateful,' she'd written, 'for any information you can give me about the mother of a girl born 'under X' on 29th July 1944, and formally adopted on 10th November 1944 by Fernand Bondel and his wife Margot Bondel (née Monier).'

Shifting in her armchair now, she looked out of the window, remembering. The milkman was coming up the

48

path, two pints of milk in his hand, one for her and one for the couple in the bedsit above. The reply, a fortnight later, had been polite but regretful: they couldn't help her.

In the meantime she'd written to the address given as her place of birth on her birth certificate. Somehow it sounded like a private house rather than a hospital, and Lucie was more than hopeful as she followed the French custom of printing her own name and address along the back flap of the envelope.

The letter came back to her in less than a week, the words 'Address unknown' in red ink across the front. It was a bitter, worrying blow.

Was it a fictitious address? Had Ray been right when he'd suggested her birth mother might have taken steps to safeguard her anonymity?

She'd sent a second letter to the town hall, asking for a list of doctors and midwives in Poitiers, intending to write to each of them in turn to ask if they recalled helping a woman give birth 'under X'. So far there had been no reply.

Recalling the other point her stepfather had made, she'd also written just over a dozen letters identical in wording to the one she'd sent to the town hall in Poitiers, sending them to towns and villages in an ever-widening circle around Poitiers.

But it was a dispiriting business. The few replies she'd received were unhelpful or negative. Lucie had the impression she was dealing with faceless bureaucrats. More and more she felt she needed to speak to real people — and that meant going to France.

What was more, the only way she could think of to trace people with the surname France was by consulting phone books, and that couldn't be done in England.

She ran the idea past her stepfather when she called him that evening prompt at six.

'I'm not looking for another mother,' she hastened to reassure him when she heard the concern in his voice. 'I'm not looking for another family. You're my family.'

Her stepfather phoned back an hour later.

'Look, I've been thinking,' he said. 'I'm going to buy you a car. A very early birthday present. Not a new one. Second-hand. But it'll give you more freedom. You won't have to rely on buses and trains.'

It was a marvellous offer. Lucie was deeply moved.

'Thank you,' she said simply.

They finalised the details. Lucie would go down to Sussex the following weekend and together they'd choose and buy a car. She'd hand in her notice at the Thieves' Kitchen, the pub where she worked while 'resting', and take the ferry across the Channel as soon afterwards as she could.

When finally she replaced the receiver, she was conscious of lurking trepidation and growing excitement. What would she find in France?

51

Change of Heart

Lucie's doorbell rang, loud in the narrow hallway, startling her out of her thoughts. She crossed to the front door and pulled it open.

'Yannick!' she cried, laughing with the pleasure of seeing him. 'Come in. I didn't realise you were in England.'

He stepped forward, favouring his left leg just a little. His arms went round her, wrapping her in a hug, and she breathed in the citrus notes of his aftershave lotion.

'I've been working on a story. A French businessman with shady dealings in the City. That's why I'm here in London.'

He held her away from him, and Lucie was conscious of his dark gaze studying her features.

'Your eyes are sparkling,' he said. 'You look happy.'

52

'I am. I learned this morning I've got a major role in the new BBC soap.' Her voice bubbled with happiness. Bar that terse letter from France, it had been a good day, she thought. And Yannick's arrival had just made it even better.

'I phoned my story in an hour ago,' he said, 'so we've both got reason to celebrate. Let me take you to Chez André. My treat.'

Half an hour later, they sat opposite each other at a small table tucked away in one corner of the best French restaurant in London.

'So,' Yannick said, 'a major role in the new soap that's going to rival 'Coronation Street'. Congratulations!' He'd ordered an expensive French pétillant, a Château Fournier d'Aucourte, and now he raised his glass and chinked it against hers. 'Margot would have been so proud of you.'

The light from the single candle on the table softened the strong lines of his face. Delicious cooking smells wafted around the two of them.

'Yes,' Lucie said quietly. She took a sip of her wine. The bubbles danced in her mouth and down her throat. 'I wish she could have been here to see it happen. She always believed I'd make it.'

Slowly twirling the stem of her glass between her fingers, she looked down at the tablecloth. Margot had always encouraged her in her ambitions, had never urged her to play it safe and take a course in shorthand typing 'just in case'. A lump formed in her throat.

Yannick's hand closed over hers, his touch warm and sure, and she looked up in surprise, almost knocking her wine glass over.

'You still miss her, of course.'

'More than I can say. When I moved to London we were always in touch, by letter, by phone.' She paused a moment, remembering. She drew in a long breath. 'So tell me what you've been doing since you went back to France,' she said. 'Dad says you've been investigating the background to stories in the news.'

'That's right. Going into greater depth.

54

I love it. It's something to get my teeth into. My next project is a series of reports on people who've broken the mould in some way, starting with a woman called Réjane d'Aucourte. Her husband makes the bubbly we're drinking. Have you heard of her?'

Lucie shook her head. His hand still covered hers, she noticed. Every now and then, the pad of his thumb stroked across her skin. As before, on the beach, she decided she rather liked the feel of it, and made no move to pull her hand away.

'Will you go back to Vietnam?'

He shrugged.

'Bernard says I don't have to decide straight away.'

'Bernard?'

'The editor of the 'Clairon Hebdomadaire'. He . . . '

The waiter hovering by their table gave a discreet cough.

'Would madame and monsieur care to order now?'

He thinks we're boyfriend and

55

girlfriend — lovers, even, she thought, conscious of the warmth that crept up over her cheeks. Now she understood why the staff had tucked them away in this quiet corner.

Her mind flashed back to the way they'd entered the restaurant. Yannick, as so often in the past, had put his arm across her shoulders, and their heads were close as he ushered her inside.

She looked at him as he gave their order. There was no way of telling if the same thought had crossed his mind, too. But he lifted his hand away from hers, and she was aware of a strange kind of loss.

As children, they'd always spent the school holidays together, either in France or in England. Then had come the years when they'd seen each other only rarely.

Yannick had gone to university and, later, she'd studied at RADA, and by the time she'd finished there, he was far away, sending reports back from the war in Vietnam.

Now, as she listened to his plans for the next few months, she found she was looking with new eyes at those dark arching eyebrows of his, the shadow of the next day's beard along the strong lines of his jaw, his even features, those beautiful eyes.

Her heart quickened its beat. For the first time, she realised, she was seeing him not as a cousin or older brother, but as a man. A very attractive man.

'Lucie . . . ' A change in his tone, difficult to pinpoint, brought her back to the here and now. 'I phoned your dad before I drove over to your bedsit. He said you intend going to France to look for your birth mother.'

'Yes. I do.'

'I don't want to see you hurt, Lucie. And you will be. You're on a wild goose chase. But you know that. I've told you, others have told you, over and over.'

There was no mistaking the concern, anger, too, in the taut lines of his face. Lucie swallowed, but her voice was clear and determined.

'I've got to try, at least.'

The waiter brought their first course, a seafood platter for each of them, and Yannick didn't reply straight away. Then he spoke firmly.

'Look, let's imagine by some fluke you do succeed in finding your birth mother. You might not like what you find. What was she when she fell pregnant with you? A wartime good-time girl? A rape victim? Mistress of some Nazi high-up? Have you thought of that?'

Horizontal collaboration, that's what they'd called it back then, she'd learned from her research at the library.

Her chin came up.

'Yes, I have. I've thought of all that. But I've still got to do it. Find my real mother, I mean.'

'Then you're a fool. A stubborn fool.'

Lucie felt shock for the space of a heartbeat as the hurtful words sank in. Her fingers fumbled as she bent her head to peel a prawn. She could have cried.

The warmth there'd been between them such a short time ago had vanished, was now nothing more than a distant memory.

She lifted her head, looked him straight in the eyes.

'You'd call yourself a realist. You'd say you were facing facts. But do you know what?' She stood up, scraping her chair back across the tiles. 'I'd rather be me: determined, positive and upbeat — even though I know I'm almost certain to fail.'

An Unexpected Kiss

'Arlette, it's lovely to see you again!' Lucie dropped her suitcase to the ground, a broad smile on her face as she wrapped her aunt in a heartfelt hug. It was so good to be back in France.

'Did you have a good journey, Lucie, *chérie*?' Arlette kissed her on both cheeks before urging her inside her second-floor apartment. 'Come on in. Have you eaten? What can I get you?'

'Yes, a brilliant journey, thanks. No problem at all with the car.'

Her father had bought her an eleven-year-old Renault Dauphine. To her delight it was a left-hand-drive, which was no doubt the reason he'd been able to pick it up at a bargain price. It was blue, with matching upholstery and white-walled tyres, and she loved it.

She'd caught the ferry early that morning and had driven down to Tours, stopping for a leisurely lunch in a small restaurant on the way.

She'd wound the car window down and the June sun had been warm on her face and bare arms. The long straight French roads with their edging of trees on either side were a delight; she'd loved every minute of the drive down.

And of course, constantly at the back of her mind was the notion that every kilometre she took deeper into France was bringing her ever closer to her birth mother.

'Sit down,' Arlette said, gesturing towards the sofa. 'Make yourself at home. I'll make us a herbal tea each, shall I? Or would you prefer coffee?'

'Let me help,' Lucie said, following her aunt into the kitchen.

'Yannick's been staying the last few days,' Arlette said, filling a saucepan with water and putting it on the stove. 'He's working on a couple of stories from round here.'

'Yannick? Oh.' Conscious of the colour spreading over her cheeks, Lucie busied herself fetching cups and a jug down from the cupboard.

All at once, the last time she and Yannick had been together was vivid in her mind. Dismayed, she realised she'd assumed he'd be in Paris. He had a one-bedroom apartment there.

'You should have told me,' she said. 'I don't want to impose. I could easily spend the night in a *chambre d'hôte*. Or go on down to Poitiers, even.' She drew in a breath. 'Does he know I'm coming?'

'You won't be imposing. And there's no problem. You'll have the guest room — I've already changed the sheets — and Yannick can have the sofa for tonight.' She paused, putting two scoops of tea in the jug and pouring hot water on top, and Lucie could see the concern in her eyes when she continued.

'He told me what happened. But try to understand, Lucie. He doesn't want to see you hurt.' She put jug, cups, and a plate of home-made strawberry tartlets on a tray. 'Anyway, enough of that. Let's go into the lounge and you can tell me all about the part you've got in the new soap.'

★ ★ ★

Half an hour later, Lucie sat back in the sofa and sighed. She felt perfectly relaxed. She smiled at her aunt. Arlette, rather, she thought with a jolt. But the older woman's warmth, her hospitality, both were so familiar, so total and unquestioning, it was hard to think of her as anyone but her aunt.

Arlette stood up, started to put the tea things back on the tray.

'I've got a pile of papers to mark. Would you mind if I left you to your own devices for a while?'

'Hey, leave that to me. I'll wash these things up.'

When she'd finished the washing-up, Lucie crossed over to the open window of the lounge. Resting her forearms on the sill, she looked out over the scene before her.

Arlette's apartment was in the centre

of Tours. The square below was as busy as ever, and the hum of human activity drifted up towards her, punctuated from time to time by the revving of a car engine, a blast on a horn, or a burst of music from a transistor radio.

Delicious aromas wafted up from the cafés and restaurants, their tables, chairs and bright parasols spreading out across the pavements.

Further away she saw the broad expanse of the river Loire, its waters smooth and tranquil from this distance, with no sign of the treacherous shifting sands beneath the surface. So much going on — she could stay watching for ever, she thought.

Suddenly, she heard the metallic chink of a key in the front door to Arlette's apartment. Lucie looked round, and Yannick was there. The breath caught in her throat.

He stood motionless, framed by the doorway, tall and broad-shouldered, looking at her. A lock of his dark hair had fallen over his forehead. He held his suit jacket slung over one shoulder, thumb hooked through the hanging loop at the back of the collar. At some stage he'd pulled the knot of his tie down and undone the top button of his shirt. His slim-fitting trousers were belted low at the waist.

Her throat was dry, and she swallowed.

'Yannick.'

'Lucie.'

For the space of an instant, neither of them moved. Then, with long strides, he crossed the room towards her, just as she swung round to face him, her back now to the window.

His hands went to her upper arms and the wool of his jacket brushed against her as he drew her to him. She was tall, but he was taller and she had to tilt her face up to his as he kissed her on both cheeks.

'Welcome to *la belle France*,' he murmured.

Letting his hands drop to his sides, he took a step backwards.

'You look beautiful.'

'So do you. Cousin,' she added, as though to remind herself.

'I'm not your cousin, though.'

The words hung in the air between them. Lucie looked down, only too aware that at some point, possibly weeks before, she'd stopped thinking of him as her cousin, saw him now as a man. A very attractive man.

Hah! A man with strong opinions, who refused to listen to another point of view, she thought with a flash of anger, her mind going back to the ugly scene in the restaurant in London.

As she'd walked out, she'd seen from the corner of her eye that he too had stood up, wincing as his injured leg knocked against the chair. He'd pulled out his wallet, was throwing notes down on the table.

'Go back and finish your meal,' she'd said.

'I'm not letting you walk home alone.' His voice was a growl.

'I'll catch a bus.'

'We're at the car. Get in.'

She wasn't the sort, normally, to let an argument fester. But she'd been so angry with him that she'd made no attempt to mend the breach. When he drew up outside her bedsit, she hadn't invited him in for a coffee, and, for all she knew, he'd gone back to France the next day.

She looked at him now.

'I want to apologise,' he said, 'for some of the things I said in the restaurant. I was — overharsh. I'm sorry.'

'I think we ought to call a truce as far as looking for my birth mother is concerned.'

'We'll never agree, so yes, it's the only sensible thing to do.'

Sensible! She almost spat the word out. Surely sometimes it was better to be illogical rather than sensible, to follow your heart and not your head.

'You're right,' she said, and tried to keep the bitterness out of her voice. 'We're never going to agree.'

She saw him suck in a breath, sensed he was going to shoot back an angry retort. But his mouth sketched a smile that didn't quite reach his eyes.

'I must have a shower before supper,' he said. 'Excuse me.'

It was only then, as he turned away and she felt the tension ease from her shoulders that she realised how tightly wound she'd been.

★ ★ ★

Supper was a salad of tomatoes and olives, crusty bread, and a selection of pungent cheeses from the crémerie.

'Delicious,' Lucie proclaimed, putting her knife down. 'I'll clear these things away, Arlette, and then I think I'll go for a walk.'

'Good idea,' Yannick said. 'I'll come with you.'

This brought an involuntary smile to her face.

'No need. Really.'

'I insist.'

A short while later they were outside, walking side by side as they crossed the

68

Place Plumereau, making for the river.

'Arlette says you're working on a couple of stories from around here,' Lucie said. The evening air was still, pleasantly cool on her bare arms. She was aware, too aware, of Yannick at her side, and took care she didn't accidentally touch him.

'That's right. One's about a woman who's hoping to become one of the few female members of parliament.'

'Oh, yes. You mentioned her before. In London.'

'The other's about a man who's self-taught but has managed to build up a multi-million-franc business for himself.'

'Both sound fascinating.'

'They are. Especially as both parties give me the impression they're hiding something.'

'Ah!' she said with a laugh. 'The intrepid reporter on the trail of a scoop.'

He turned to look at her, and his eyes too sparkled with laughter.

'Got it in one.'

After that, things were easier between them, and they walked on in a comfortable silence broken only by the occasional comment from one or the other.

The evening sun slanted ribbons of shimmering light across the smooth water of the Loire. The sounds of cars and people seemed very distant. Close by, a water vole ran scurrying for cover, while a quiet 'plop' told them a fish had bobbed its head above the surface of the river before bobbing down again.

'So what are your plans for the immediate future?' Yannick asked, looking out over the water.

'I'm going to go down to Poitiers, speak to former neighbours, go to the town hall, try and trace the address that's on my birth certificate — and take it from there.

'No comment?' she added when he said nothing.

He shook his head, and turned so that they stood face to face, very close, almost touching.

'Lucie . . . ' There was uncharacteristic hesitation in his voice, and Lucie was conscious of a tightness in her chest.

She watched, heart beating rapidly, as he brought his hand up. He stroked a strand of her hair behind her ear, brushed his knuckles across her cheek, touched the pad of his thumb to the corner of her mouth. And all the time, his eyes were intent on hers.

'Stay strong, Lucie,' he said at last. 'I rather think you're going to need all your strength in the days and weeks to come.'

Slowly, so slowly, he bent his head towards hers, and she found she was holding her breath as his lips touched hers in the lightest of kisses.

Good to be Back

This part of Poitiers had barely changed over the years, Lucie thought, as she rounded the corner. She came to a halt and stood, simply watching.

Before her, on the other side of the cobbled street, was the chemist's shop where she'd spent the first five years of her life, its green neon cross flashing as it had always done. Pots of flowers spilled out of the florist's shop next door on to the narrow pavement.

On its other side, where the street sloped uphill, a stand of newspapers and two posters giving the day's headlines advertised the newsagent's.

It was mid-morning and cars, forced to wait behind a delivery van, clogged the side of the street nearest her. Diesel and petrol fumes drifted upwards, and the sounds of impatient horns filled the air. A scooter clattered over the cobbles, dodging into the oncoming lane to pass the waiting cars.

Shoppers went by, in and out of shops, some strolling, some hurrying, and all of them, Lucie thought, speaking at the tops of their voices. She smiled, happiness easing over her. She'd spent her early years here and it was good to be back.

There was a second reason for that feeling of happiness, of course. She touched her fingers to her lips, remembering Yannick's kiss the evening before.

He'd already left before she set out on her 90-minute drive down to Poitiers that morning. She had no idea when she'd see him again.

For an instant the cars were at a standstill and Lucie seized the opportunity to zigzag between them as she headed for the newsagent's. It was a small shop crammed full. There were piles of newspapers on the floor and on the counter, displays of magazines on wide shelves on Lucie's left and fountain pens, bottles of ink and writing paper neatly arranged on her right.

'Lucie!' With a murmured apology to the customer she was serving, Géraldine Bonenfant came round from behind the counter, wrapped Lucie in a hug and kissed her on both cheeks. 'You're looking so well. How lovely to see you. Just wait there. I'll get Claude down.' She gave her customer his newspaper and change, at the same time pushing aside the curtain behind her. 'Claude,' she called out. 'She's here. Come on down.'

Moments later, Lucie heard the rapid pounding of feet on lino-covered stairs and she was enveloped in a second hug by Géraldine's husband, Claude.

'Come on through,' Géraldine said. 'Claude'll mind the shop. I'll make us some coffee.' She ushered Lucie past the curtain and into the kitchen and gestured to her to sit at the table. A mouth-watering aroma of chicken simmering in red wine on the stove filled the room. 'I was so sorry to hear about Margot.'

Lucie expelled her breath in a long sigh.

'It was so sudden, so fast.' Her stepfather had written to Géraldine and Claude about Margot's illness and its sorry conclusion.

The two families had kept in touch over the years, and her mother and stepfather had always found time to call on her former neighbours during their frequent visits to France. Until she moved away from the parental home, Lucie, too, had spent most summer holidays with her parents in France, often staying with her aunt.

'I still can't get over it. Dad went back to work just days after the funeral. Using work as a comfort blanket.' She fell silent, lost in thought, and was grateful that Géraldine busied herself grinding beans and percolating the coffee.

She'd done the same as her step-father, of course, Lucie realised, working in the pub near her bedsit all the hours she could and writing to town halls in and around Poitiers in her spare time.

The rich smell of strong coffee brought

her back to the present. Géraldine had poured it into the tall handleless cups the French called mazagrans that always looked to Lucie like jumbo-sized egg cups.

Géraldine sat down opposite Lucie and pushed one of the cups across to her.

'What you said, in your letter, about Margot and Fernand . . . ' She spoke hesitantly, clearly unsure what to say.

Lucie had written the week before saying she'd like to come and see her and asking her if she could find somewhere for her to stay. She'd also said in the letter that she'd been adopted, though she hadn't gone into any further detail.

'I just couldn't believe it.' Géraldine shook her head.

'You had no idea?'

'No.' Géraldine took a cube of sugar from the box on the table and popped it in her coffee. 'You were two, I think, when we bought this place.' She smiled. 'Walking around on those long legs of yours — you were tall even then — and talking nineteen to the dozen.' She shook her head again, the smile fading. 'Neither of them ever let on they'd adopted you.'

Lucie was silent again, considering.

'Were they friendly with any doctors, Géraldine?'

The older woman reached across the table and put her hand over Lucie's, as if sensing the question was an important one.

'Fernand was a chemist, Mélu.' Her use of the diminutive came, as always, as a shock. Géraldine was one of the few who remembered that her name was not in fact Lucie but Mélusine — the name, according to Margot, that her birth mother had chosen for her.

'He and Margot knew most if not all the doctors in Poitiers,' she went on. 'Whether they were friends with any of them, I couldn't tell you.'

Lucie bit her lip, unable to hide her disappointment.

'I'm sorry I haven't been able to help

77

more,' Géraldine said.

'No, don't apologise. I . . . '

'But I have found you somewhere to stay. It's with a Madame Guellerin. She's a widow, retired. She's not on the phone but she's expecting you some time this morning. I'll take you round there.'

All at once Lucie felt better. It made sense to have a base in Poitiers. Although Arlette was more than willing for her to stay with her in Tours, it would be a long way for her to drive each day. She swallowed the rest of her coffee and stood up.

'Thank you so much. That's marvellous.'

She moved back out to the shop and kissed Claude goodbye while Géraldine ran upstairs to fetch her handbag.

She smiled when the older woman reappeared.

'The magazine editors here seem to have a fixation about Jackie Kennedy,' she said, gesturing at the array of magazines.

'Ah well, we've got our own home-grown Jackie K now. Here.' Géraldine picked up that week's edition of the 'Clairon Hebdomadaire' and handed it to Lucie. She flicked through until she came to a full-page photo of an elegant woman in her 40s, long hair brushed into a smooth French pleat, diamond studs in her ears. She had a smile that reached her eyes, Lucie thought, giving her that rare combination, a mix of grace and warmth.

'She lives, oh, fifty, sixty kilometres north of here,' Géraldine said.

But it was the name on the opposite page that had caught Lucie's attention.

'I know the man who wrote this article,' she said with a rush of pride. 'He's my — ' She broke off, colouring as she remembered his kiss, feather-light, infinitely tender.

She drew in a shaky breath. No. Definitely not her cousin.

High Hopes

Lucie took to Viviane Guellerin straight away and hoped the feeling was mutual. Welcoming and considerate, in her 60s or perhaps her 70s, her new landlady bustled around with a vigour that belied her age.

She showed Lucie her room, which faced south, letting the sun stream in, and insisted the young woman have lunch with her.

'The price I've given you is for a month with full board,' she said. 'You can stay all summer if you want.'

Two hours later after a delicious meal, Lucie set out, a spring in her step as she walked along in the June sunshine. She smiled as the light breeze ruffled her hair. She was on a quest, her hopes were high.

The post office had returned the letter she'd sent to 2 impasse de la

Gare, saying the address was unknown. But was it the whole street that didn't exist, or simply number 2? Were there a number 1 and a number 3 Station Close? That was what she intended finding out that afternoon.

It was the main entrance building of the station that caught and held Lucie's eye. Standing on the other side of the road, she looked across, beyond the car park to the strong vertical lines in concrete and glass so beloved of post-war architects, and could see the glimmer of a solution to her mystery.

At the far end of the station concourse was a café, its bright parasols inviting her over. Someone there would be able to help her, she was sure. Lucie crossed the road and threaded her way past the zigzagging lines of cars parked on the station forecourt.

'A citron pressé, please,' she said, taking a seat beneath one of the parasols. The waiter was in his 50s and Lucie felt more optimistic than ever.

'Tell me,' she went on as he started to

81

turn away, 'the station looks as if it's been rebuilt fairly recently.'

'That's right. It was destroyed in the war. Bombed by our so-called allies,' he added with more than a hint of bitterness.

'I'm looking for 2 impasse de la Gare,' Lucie said when he came back and set her freshly squeezed lemon juice down on the table in front of her.

'Ah, the clinic.'

Lucie's heart leaped. So the address did exist.

'The clinic?'

'The Clinique du Bon Endroit.'

The clinic of the good place. Lucie found herself smiling again. An auspicious name, it couldn't be otherwise.

'Is it near here?' she asked.

The waiter shook his head and started to move towards the people taking their places at a nearby table.

'It got bombed too. It doesn't exist any more. Excuse me, mademoiselle.'

Lucie watched him make his way across to the other table and slowly sipped her citron pressé as she reflected on what he'd said. So 2 impasse de la Gare wasn't a private house, the house where her mother might have lived, and that was disappointing.

Disappointing, too, was the fact that the clinic was no longer there. She couldn't simply go in and ask to speak to someone who had worked there in 1944. On a positive note, however, the address wasn't fictitious, as Lucie had suspected when her letter had been returned to her.

It was probable that the Clinique du Bon Endroit was indeed her place of birth. It was a solid fact she could surely build on.

★ ★ ★

The spring was back in Lucie's step as she made her way the next morning to the town hall in Poitiers, an ornate fairytale palace when contrasted with the austere modern lines of the station. It was another beautiful day. How could her hopes be other than high?

She'd made some progress the day before. Not much, but some. Perhaps today she'd learn a little more, would place another piece in the jigsaw puzzle.

She ran lightly up the steps and through tall, arched doors into the entrance hall. Ahead of her a gleaming white marble staircase soared, branching into two as it neared the first floor.

The woman at reception sent her through a door on her right and along a corridor. Lucie knocked on the door marked 'Official records'.

'Come in.' The woman who called out looked close to retirement. Her hair, pulled into a bun at her nape, held streaks of silver at the temples. When she saw Lucie come in she closed the buff-coloured folder on her desk and pushed it to one side. 'Sit down, mademoiselle. What can I do for you?'

'I was born under X here in Poitiers in 1944. I'm trying to trace my mother.'

The official sat back in her chair, clasping her hands together on the desk.

'I'm sorry. I can't help you.' Her tone was courteous but firm. 'That's the whole point of being born under X. The records don't give the mother's name. She remains anonymous.'

'Yes, I know.' Lucie's mouth was dry. The woman had told her nothing new. It was what she, or a colleague of hers, had written in reply to Lucie's letter a few weeks before. She ran her tongue over her lips. 'But I've got a surname. It might be my mother's name too.'

Even before she'd finished speaking, the other woman was shaking her head.

'No. I'm afraid not. When a child is born under X, the registrar, or the child's mother, gives him or her three Christian names, and the third one becomes the child's surname.'

'Oh.' The information came at her like a punch, driving the air from her lungs. With a shake of her head, she recalled Margot's letter. Her adoptive mother had said the names Mélusine Jeanne had been chosen by her birth mother.

So it must have been the registrar who had chosen the name France, the name that was given as her surname in her adoption papers. What she'd hoped was a clue to her mother's identity was no such thing.

She squared her shoulders, knew she had to try a different tack.

'Is it possible my mother left some message, some indication of who she was?'

'Nowadays, that might be the case sometimes. It's something mothers are encouraged to do, in fact. But it never happened back then.' She paused. The look in her eyes as they searched Lucie's features was kind. 'The war was still going on. This part of France was occupied.' Another pause. 'Don't you think it might be best to let sleeping dogs lie, mademoiselle?'

For a long silent moment, their eyes met. What the woman had not said hung between them like a ghost from the past. Her stepfather, Arlette, Yannick, everyone else she'd spoken to

— one way or another each one of them had issued the same warning.

'I've got to do it, though. Keep on looking for her, I mean.' Lucie spoke with a quiet conviction that ruled out any other course of action.

'Yes, I understand,' the older woman said at last, and it occurred to Lucie that she did indeed understand.

'Can I give you my name and phone number?' Lucie said, somehow encouraged. 'Just in case you do find something in your archives?' She watched as the woman noted down her name and Arlette's phone number and pushed it under the blotter on her desk.

'One last thing,' the official said. 'You were born under X so best take your place of birth with a pinch of salt.' When Lucie frowned, she added, 'You might not have been born here in Poitiers.'

Falling in Love?

The woman's words at the records office, had thrown Lucie right back to the beginning. She didn't have a surname that might have been her mother's, and she possibly didn't have the right place of birth either.

She sat at the desk in her room, writing home. In letters to two friends in London, she'd tried to remain upbeat. But now, as she drew another piece of notepaper towards her, she knew it would be harder to hide her emotions from her stepfather, and it was with a heavy heart that she picked up her fountain pen.

The ringing of the doorbell mingled with the shouts of children playing in the street below. She half-heard madame Guellerin's bustling '*J'arrive, j'arrive*' as she went to answer it, followed by the familiar deep tones of a voice she knew so well, and her stomach did a crazy flip-flop.

'Yannick!' She pushed the cap back on her pen, scraped her chair back, and raced downstairs.

He stood in the doorway, and she was reminded of how she'd first seen him two days before, and again the breath caught in her throat.

'Yannick. What a lovely surprise. But how did you know where to find me?'

'Ah, good,' Lucie's landlady broke in, 'the two of you know each other. Go out into the garden, go on. There's a bench out there. Make the most of the sunshine.' And with that, she turned and headed back to the kitchen.

'My mother gave me your address,' Yannick said moments later. 'I phoned her from Bordeaux.'

'Oh, yes. Of course.' After giving Arlette's phone number to the employee at Poitiers Town Hall, good manners — if nothing else — had dictated she should phone her aunt and put her in the picture. 'Bordeaux?'

'The self-taught multi-millionaire. Francs, not pounds.'

He fell silent, and Lucie was conscious of a certain awkwardness between the two of them. He wore a black short-sleeved T-shirt above slim-fitting trousers. She watched as he massaged the calf of his left leg before sitting back, to all appearances perfectly relaxed, his arms stretched either side of him along the back of the bench. The scent of honeysuckle was all around.

'You want to know how I got on,' she said at last.

He didn't answer straight away.

'Only if you want to tell me,' he said slowly.

She looked at him, taking in the strong lines of his face, saw the faint frown that creased his brow, the concern in his eyes, and she knew she did want to tell him. And so she did, spilling out all her disappointment, her thwarted hopes.

He didn't gloat or say, 'I told you so' or call her an idiot for even thinking she might get a positive result after only a day or two. Instead, he listened, intently, throwing in a comment or a question from time to time, and she was grateful.

At one moment his arm curved round her shoulder, drawing her to him, and she could have cried, cocooned and comforted as she was by his warmth and strength.

He left soon after, saying he intended spending the night at his mother's before travelling on to Paris. But that brief visit set the pattern for the next few weeks.

Whenever he was in the area — and work seemed to bring him more and more often to this part of France — he'd call by in the early evening. If she wanted to talk about her day, he listened, was quietly supportive. If she didn't, then he didn't press her, and they talked about something else.

When Lucie's landlady started referring to him as 'your young man', Lucie protested that he wasn't. But she had to admit he'd become a good friend to her. Her disappointments were so frequent, the answers she received to her enquiries so unremittingly negative, she wasn't sure at times how she could have coped if he hadn't been there.

★ ★ ★

'Yannick, you're not limping any more. Your leg must have healed up completely.'

It was another early evening, and the two of them were walking side by side, making for the park a short distance from her landlady's house.

'It has. I was lucky.' He stooped and picked up a stone. With a vicious twist of his arm he sent it skittering low over the cobbles. 'Luckier than lots of others. It didn't kill me. And it wasn't napalm.'

Lucie said nothing, remembering their shock the day she, Ray and Margot had received Arlette's letter.

Yannick had been with an American patrol, her aunt had written, when they'd come under attack. Grenades had gone off, killing two marines and wounding several others. Fragments of rock and splinters of wood had thudded into the calf and thigh of Yannick's left leg, she'd said, and he was being flown home to France for treatment.

That first letter had been brief. Subsequent letters had given more detail. But it had been a harrowing time for her aunt. For them all, Lucie recalled.

'If you go back to Vietnam, what's to prevent something like it from happening again?'

He must have heard the way her voice caught for he swung round to face her.

'Nothing,' he said, taking her hands in both his. His grip was firm and warm. 'There's nothing to stop it happening again.'

'Then why do you do it, expose yourself to danger like that?'

He paused before replying, and Lucie saw that his dark eyes were looking inward.

'Because when I'm out there, I'm a witness. An independent voice. I'm not American, and I'm not Vietnamese. I

93

can report objectively on what I see, give an unbiased account.'

There was no doubting his sincerity, and Lucie felt her heart swell with pride in him.

'Think of the last war,' he went on. 'The Nazis committed all sorts of atrocities, but it was all hidden away. Very few people knew — and even fewer were talking about any of it.'

'The massacres, the death camps — it all came out in the end, though.' Yannick's expression was grim.

'That was the price they paid for losing. I've got no doubt the winners, too, did things, awful things, and they've never been made public.'

'Maybe one day they will be,' Lucie said, jolted by his vehemence, and by the edge of cynicism in his tone.

'That's why I do what I do. The soldiers on the ground can't question the orders they're given. Discipline would break down if they did. So we journalists are the ones who call people to account.

'Because of us, politicians have to explain their decisions, and generals have to justify their actions.'

'So you are going back,' Lucie said unhappily. She glanced down, unable to look him in the eyes any more. She felt as if a vast, empty gulf were opening up before her.

'Lucie, sweet.' Letting go one of her hands, he touched her chin with his index finger, tilting it up so she had to meet his gaze. 'I haven't decided yet. I was out there two years. You could say I've done my stint.'

'You have, yes,' she said, conscious it was a faintly ridiculous remark to make.

He smiled.

'I must admit I like what I'm doing here. Going into greater depth, asking questions, not taking things at face value.'

'Sceptical . . . cynical . . . Being an investigative journalist suits you right down to the ground.'

He laughed.

'It's not so different from what I was

doing out there. Come on,' he added, 'let's get to the park.'

She sucked in a breath when he put his arm across her shoulders, as he so often did, and drew her against the lean strength of his body. As they continued along the pavement, she caught only snatches of what he was saying.

' . . . finished for the time being with the multi-millionaire . . . Réjane d'Aucourte . . . couple of leads I'll be following up . . .'

Her attention was elsewhere.

He was principled and brave. He comforted and supported her even though he was convinced she was on a wild goose chase. He was good-looking. And he set her senses alight.

Yes, she thought, and her pulses sped into a faster beat, she was in danger of falling in love with Yannick Savaton.

Dispiriting News

Lucie parked her car beneath one of the lime trees that lined the square in the centre, of the village of Merton-les-Bois. Getting out, she looked across at the *mairie*, the town hall.

It wasn't a large building, probably just two rooms on each of its two storeys. Its stone walls, the colour of thick cream, looked dull and worn in the afternoon light.

Heavy clouds had massed, covering the sun, and bringing a chill to the air. She pulled a cardigan on over the gently draped 1940s crepe she wore, another jumble sale bargain, its pattern of posies of flowers forming bright splashes of pink, green and yellow on the black background.

The grey of the clouds mirrored the grey of her mood, Lucie decided as she checked that the doors of the car were all locked. She had to stay optimistic, she thought, but it was becoming more and more difficult.

She was conscious she was fighting a growing despondency, the sense she was getting nowhere, making no progress.

Lucie paused by the car, thinking back. She'd started out with great optimism, convinced that if she saw people in person she'd get more positive results. But the official at the town hall in Poitiers had set the pattern.

Apart from the previous weekend when she had driven to Tours to stay with her aunt, Lucie had spent her time enquiring at the town halls in the towns and villages surrounding Poitiers.

Each visit, Lucie thought, squaring her shoulders and crossing towards the *mairie* of Merton-les-Bois, had produced a variation on the same depressing theme — they were very sorry but they couldn't help her. She'd left her name and her aunt's phone number each time, but deep down she knew she didn't expect to hear from any of them.

The notice on the door said the *mairie* was only open between two and four on Mondays and Thursdays. Lucie glanced at her wristwatch. A quarter to four, and it was Thursday, she was in luck. A good omen, she wondered, opening the door.

A red arrow and the words *Secrétariat — Salle de Réunion* indicated she should climb the stairs that reared up, steep and narrow, immediately in front of her. At the top she could hear the clatter of a typewriter and knocked on the door on her right.

The sound of fingers hammering out a regular rhythm on typewriter keys didn't stop or even slow as Lucie went in. The office was almost as gloomy as the stairwell and she needed a second or two for her eyes to adjust. A long table, chairs lined up on each side of it, dominated the room. A portrait of General de Gaulle looked down from the fire breast.

'Yes?'

Lucie looked across the room. A middle-aged woman sat at a table by the window, her fingers busy still at the keys. A cigarette burned in the ashtray beside her, a thin thread of smoke drifting lazily up to the ceiling.

The woman's tone was that of someone wearied by yet another interruption. Lucie bristled with annoyance.

'I wrote to you a few weeks ago. My name's Lucie Curtis,' she said, looking at the woman with open curiosity.

This must be the author of the letter she'd received the day she'd learned she'd got the part in the new soap, the unhelpful letter that had confirmed her in her decision to pursue her enquiries in France.

'Oh, yes, I remember.' The secretary slammed back the carriage return. She wore a white blouse above a navy skirt, and a lighter blue scarf tied in a large bow at her neck. Her nail varnish matched the vivid pink of her lipstick while her short dark hair, backcombed into a smooth bouffant, looked sadly out of date. 'You gave details about a child, wanted information about the mother. You're the child?'

Lucie nodded.

'We don't give out that sort of information by post, I'm afraid. I'd be typing all day if I answered all the letters we receive here.'

Lucie's hands clenched, irritation threatening to turn to anger. She couldn't believe what she'd just heard.

'I'm here in person,' she said, forcing all emotion out of her voice. 'You won't need to write me a letter. So maybe you can help me now.'

'I'm not sure how.' The secretary picked up her cigarette, drawing on it and blowing the smoke out straight away so that it billowed around her face. 'Didn't you say you were adopted?' Lucie nodded again. 'Well, then,' the secretary resumed her typing, 'details of your birth will have been changed. Only your adoptive parents will be mentioned. The original record will have been destroyed.'

'What?' It was difficult to hear above the noise of the typewriter. 'I don't understand.'

The secretary pulled her work out of the typewriter, separating it into paper, carbon and flimsy. She stood up and glanced at her watch before looking across at Lucie.

'I'd try the adoption agencies if I were you.'

Lucie went back to Poitiers town hall the next morning.

'But you didn't say you'd been adopted.' It was the same person as before. Her tone was one of mild reproof. 'What happens is this. When you are adopted, there's a court ruling ordering a new certificate to be drawn up. Your adoptive parents are the only parents mentioned on this new certificate and in our official records.'

'And the original record is destroyed,' Lucie said, echoing the words of the secretary in the town hall at Merton-les-Bois.

The other woman shook her head.

'Not destroyed, but as good as. It will have been struck out and put in the vaults.'

'The vaults?' A tiny spark of hope flared. 'It's still here somewhere, in this building? Can I see it?'

'No. No-one can.' She spoke with finality and the brief spark of hope flickered out.

Lucie paused. It was as if she'd come up against a brick wall. She didn't want to leave the matter there, but was uncertain how to continue.

'So can you tell me,' she said at last, 'what my original certificate would have been like?'

The official sighed.

'There'd be the date, time and place of birth. Your three Christian names. The fact you're a girl. Next the name, profession and address of the person who was reporting the birth, someone who had been present. Normally it's a relative, but in your case it could be a doctor, a midwife maybe.'

Another name, another possible clue as to her mother's identity. Lucie bit back on her frustration. What she would give to get a look at that certificate.

103

'What about my mother? Whereabouts is the 'X' in place of her name?' she asked.

The woman shook her head again.

'There is no 'X'.' She spoke kindly, as though unwilling to break bad news. 'There's no mention of the mother at all.'

World of Their Own

Much later that day Lucie sat at the table by the window of the room she was renting from Viviane Guellerin.

Fountain pen in hand, she looked down on the street below. Noisy and bustling with activity by day, it was more or less silent now in the gathering gloom of dusk. She'd pulled the window open and the scent of honeysuckle from Madame Guellerin's front garden came in on the evening air that ruffled the heavy net curtains.

Lucie was bringing her stepfather up to date but every word, it seemed, had to be pulled out of her. Even when recounting factual information such as her fruitless enquiries so far, or the suggestion that she try adoption agencies, which had given her a little spur of hope, she had to swallow against the ache in her throat.

'I suppose I've had a good day really, Dad,' she continued writing. 'So why do I feel so down? Part of the trouble is, I keep thinking about my real mother. For all I know, she's living here in Poitiers. I might have passed her on the street. If I see a woman in her 40s or 50s I catch myself thinking: Is that her? Does she look like me? Is she married? Have I got brothers or sisters? So many questions and I just feel I'm never going to find the answers. That's why I'm feeling so depressed, I suppose.'

There was more to it of course, something Lucie could only acknowledge in her bleakest moments, a source of shame made worse by the look in the eyes of some of the officials she'd spoken to.

She bowed her head, pressing the tips of her fingers hard into her forehead, moving them slowly from side to side. She had questions without answers, questions that cut to the quick, cruel stabs of pain that nothing could ease.

Why had her mother rejected her?

Had she been such an ugly baby? Had she cried a lot? What had been so wrong with her that her own mother had wanted rid of her?

Lucie looked round as the whisper of a noise told her madame Guellerin's cat had come into the room. Réglisse, which meant Liquorice, black as coal and with huge lime-green eyes, stalked across the room on long, rangy legs. The cat leaned her weight against Lucie's ankles and purred when she reached down, absent-mindedly stroking the smooth fur.

All at once she felt guilty, burdening her stepfather with her negative thoughts. She forced herself to finish on an opti-mistic note, telling him her plans to drive up to Tours and spend another weekend with her aunt. Finally she folded the sheets of paper and slid them into an airmail envelope.

With a little mew, Réglisse stretched up on her hind legs and pushed her nose against Lucie's knee.

The tears that had threatened spilled over at last, and Lucie scooped the cat up in her arms and buried her face in the soft fur. Plagued by doubts, making minimal progress, far from the people she loved, she'd never felt so wretched.

The clatter of pans and the aroma of tomatoes simmering reached her from the kitchen below. Her landlady was cooking their supper. Tomato soup. It was getting late, she thought. Six-thirty. Seven. Yannick wouldn't be coming to the house tonight. A fresh wave of despondency washed over her.

He came two or three times a week to Viviane Guellerin's house, sometimes more often. They'd sit on the bench in the garden beneath the honeysuckle, or walk side by side to the river or the park, or go for a short drive in his car or hers.

He drove a sporty-looking Peugeot 403, dark green with a black soft-top, that was ten years old and dented at each corner. It had clearly seen better days.

'What do you expect? I live in Paris,' he'd said with a laugh. 'And I've been abroad the last few years. No point in getting something newer just for it to languish in the garage.'

Lucie smiled at the memory, and buried her face again in Réglisse's fur. Though he rarely said so in as many words, Yannick still considered her search to be a hopeless task, she knew.

Even so, he was there when she needed him, a shoulder to cry on, a listening ear to confide in. He didn't believe in what she was doing but he was willing to support her anyway. She wasn't sure she could have coped without him.

Yes, she recognised, not for the first time, she owed him a lot. And she was close, very close, to falling in love with him.

The doorbell rang, and her heart gave a crazy lurch. Yannick, it had to be him. The cat leaped from her arms on to the desk as Lucie jumped to her feet.

She raced down the stairs, pulled open the door, and emotion flooded through her.

'Yannick!' She saw him frown when he caught sight of her, and she moved towards him. His arms went round her, drawing her to him, holding her tight. 'Oh, Yannick.'

'Lucie, sweetheart,' he murmured, rocking her gently from side to side.

'I've had the most awful couple of days.' Her voice, muffled against his shoulder, was thick with tears.

As he led her to the bench beneath the honeysuckle, his arms around her still, she poured out all her anger and frustration, her disappointment and self-doubt. And all the while he listened, soothed, murmured quiet words of comfort.

When she could cry no more, she raised her head and managed a small smile.

'I'm sorry.'

'Don't be sorry.' His hand went to the back of her head, drawing it back down to his shoulder. 'I only wish I could help you more.'

'I'm getting nowhere. All these weeks

and I'm no further forward.' She fell silent, aware she was stepping into dangerous territory, for Yannick, of course, was convinced she never would get anywhere in her search for her birth mother.

'Look at me,' he said gently, and when she lifted her head, he reached up and brushed the pad of his index finger under each of her eyes in turn, smoothing away the tears. 'What do you say, you put your glad rags on, and we'll go dancing?'

'I don't . . .'

'Get away from all this. Just for tonight.'

Still she hesitated, but then she smiled. 'Yes, why not?' All at once his suggestion seemed spot-on.

★ ★ ★

Fifteen minutes later, she ran back downstairs and out into the garden. She wore her best dress, one she'd bought new, admittedly in the sales, a sleeveless slim-fitting shift in burned orange that ended several inches above the knee.

Yannick gave a low whistle.

'You look lovely.'

She laughed.

'So do you.' Tall, dark and handsome, she thought, her gaze moving from his almost black hair and strong-boned face, past his grey and white striped shirt open at the neck, to his charcoal grey trousers, belted low at the waist. She smiled. 'Shall we go?'

It was a warm evening, and the air was still. Yannick took her hand as they went downhill, making for the river, and that too seemed just right.

As they drew nearer, they heard the rhythmic beat of a set of drums, the twang of electric guitars and a man and a woman belting out a Johnny Hallyday number.

Nearer still, and they caught the sounds of laughter and many voices.

The dance was being held in the open air, close to the water's edge. People were standing, or sitting on the benches placed on either side of trestle tables, or had taken to the dance floor, a large square of parquet which held the band at one end.

'Would mademoiselle care to dance?' Yannick asked.

Lucie laughed.

'Mademoiselle would.'

It was fun, enormous fun. They were part of a crowd of people intent on enjoying themselves, and the mood was catching. Lucie faced Yannick, a huge smile on her face, on his too, as they threw themselves into the twist and the mashed potato.

They danced to songs by Johnny Hallyday, Eddy Mitchell, Sheila, countless others, and she felt her spirits soar, her frustrations and disappointments, her lack of progress for the moment forgotten.

'Thank you for bringing me here,' she said a long while later, smiling happily. 'It's just what I needed.'

The two of them sat at a bench just metres away from the river bank, each sipping a glass of a light local wine and sharing the punnet of fried freshwater fish, the size of whitebait, that had been placed on the table in front of them.

He smiled back.

'Good. I'm glad.'

The band struck up a slow ballad.

'Come on.' Taking her hand, he drew her to her feet and led her back on to the dance floor.

He gathered her to him, his hands low at her waist, pulling her against the length of his body, setting her pulse racing. She clasped her hands behind his neck and closed her eyes, nestling her head in the crook where his collar bone started.

It felt so good. So right. The other dancers were forgotten. Only she and Yannick existed, swaying to the slow beat of the music.

He smelled of soap and she pressed a kiss to the skin of his neck. He made a sound something like a groan, deep inside his throat, and his lips were on hers, fierce and demanding, his hand coming up to tangle in her hair.

All at once there was a charge in the air. Lucie didn't know how the evening was going to end, knew only that she didn't want it to end for a long, long time.

Pleasure rippled through her. She was in a world of sensation. The rasp of his jaw, the salt taste of his skin on her tongue, the power of his body against hers, only they mattered.

'Lucie . . . ' Still keeping her in the circle of his arms, he drew a little apart. 'Lucie, come with me to Paris. Tonight. To my apartment.'

She saw the intensity in his eyes, heard the urgency in his voice, and her heart leaped. It was what she too wanted, more than anything in the world.

A smile of pure joy lit his face as he pulled her to him, enfolding her in his arms, pressing kisses to her hair, her nose, her mouth.

'We'll collect your things from Madame Guellerin,' he said, between kisses. 'She won't mind if you don't finish the month with her.'

Lucie stilled. What was he saying?

'I've got to be back here Monday. I've got adoption agencies to visit.'

'No, come with me to Paris. There's nothing here in Poitiers for you.'

'But . . . ' Conscious of the sudden chill inching its way into her bones, she couldn't finish.

'Lucie, my sweet, it's time to forget this . . . ' He broke off in mid-sentence.

'This what?' She twisted herself out of his embrace. 'This obsession? This nonsense?' She flung the words at him. 'Is that what you were going to say? That's what you really think, isn't it?' His support in the previous weeks had made her think he'd begun to understand her point of view. But he hadn't. Not at all, she thought, tears filling her eyes.

Other dancers paused an instant to look at the two of them before moving off again. She barely noticed. She didn't hear the music any more. She faced him, her whole being taut with a brittle anger.

He reached out, seemed to think better of it, and let his hand drop to his side. His face was like stone, his expression unreadable.

'It is an obsession. It is nonsense.' Emotion tugged at the corner of his mouth. 'And it's making you desperately unhappy.'

117

A Glimmer of Hope

'There's nothing you can say that would interest me, Yannick.'

Lucie's voice was hard, her expression stony. But tears were close to the surface. She stood in the doorway of her landlady's house, and he was no more than a metre away.

She could have reached out to touch him. But she didn't. And wouldn't, ever again, she thought, stepping back a pace, ready to shut the door on him before the tears spilled over.

He brought his hand up, placing the flat of his palm against the wood of the door, stopping her.

'You didn't read my letters.' Both tone and action spoke of a determination as hard and implacable as her own.

'No.' She hadn't even taken them out of their envelopes, had simply torn them up and thrown them away.

Ten days had passed since that evening by the river. Yannick had insisted on seeing her home.

'This is Poitiers, not London,' she'd snapped. 'I don't need an escort.'

'Even so, I'm coming with you.'

They'd walked back to Madame Guellerin's in silence, side by side, not touching. At the door, she'd turned.

'I don't want to see you again, Yannick,' she said. 'If you can't support me in something as important to me as this, then there's no future for us.'

The words hung in the air between them. She wouldn't cry. Not yet. She saw emotion tug at his mouth, just as it had down by the river, and she was gripped by a sense of unreality. How could this be happening?

The two of them should have been heading fast along the roads to Paris, excitement fizzing between them.

'As you wish,' he said, the words heavy, as though drained of all spirit. His hand, closing round her upper arm, gave her a brief squeeze. 'You know how to get in touch with me if . . . '

But he left the sentence unfinished. His hand dropped to his side and he swung away. Wordlessly, she watched him take the few paces down the path and out on to the pavement, and touched the place on her arm where his hand, warm and firm, had been. She had, she knew, lost something infinitely precious that night.

But it could be no other way.

She saw him now look away for a long moment, pushing his fingers in a short, angry movement through his hair, before turning his dark eyes on her again.

'I won't keep you long. I'm on my way to interview Réjane d'Aucourte.'

His hair gleamed in the midday sun. A lock of it had fallen across his forehead. How she longed to smooth it back in place.

'Please go, Yannick.'

'I've found a young woman born under X like you. I thought you might like to meet her, talk with her.'

'So she too can tell me how impossible my search will be?' A tear did fall then as she flung the words at him. She'd spent another fruitless morning, this time contacting doctors who might — just — remember a colleague who'd helped a woman give birth under X over 20 years before.

But it had been hopeless. Hopeless, hopeless, hopeless. She knew it. Knew, too, that she was getting close to the end of her tether.

He sucked in a breath.

'No. Not at all.'

Lucie stilled.

'What are you saying? That she found her birth mother? How?' Fierce joy sped through her. It wasn't hopeless. It was possible.

'She'd put a small ad in 'Vos Confessions', one of those magazines that specialise in true life stories . . . '

'I've seen them in the shops.'

' . . . just over a year ago, saying she was looking for her birth mother. That's how I found her, looking through the

121

small ads. I contacted her and quite a few others who'd put similar ads in magazines.'

'And she found her birth mother?' The question was no more than a breath.

'Here's her address. She's not on the phone.' He held out a slip of paper. 'Write to her, meet her. Find out what her story is.'

Lucie took the paper with hands that shook. An address in Angoulême. Not too far. She could drive there. 'Thank you.'

'But, Lucie . . . ' Something in his voice made her look up. His expression was grave. 'I contacted eighty-five people and got replies from eighty-three of them. Of those eighty-three, she's the only one who found her birth mother.'

★ ★ ★

Four days later, Lucie set out at the wheel of her Renault Dauphine. She'd arranged to meet Solange Perron in the

Café des Arts in the centre of the town of Angoulême.

The sun was shining, and she was in a buoyant mood, feeling more positive than she had for days, weeks. Though born under X, Solange Perron had succeeded in finding her birth mother. It was possible. And if she could do it, Lucie could, too.

A pair of swallows, flying low, looped the loop in front of her car, and she laughed. A good omen, surely.

She found the café, and Solange, with no problem. It was Sunday, and the church bells were ringing.

'Yannick — Monsieur Savaton — told me you put an ad in 'Vos Confessions' about a year ago.'

'That's right.'

'Could you tell me about it? Why then? Why not before? And what happened?' The questions spilled out. She couldn't help it. 'Tell me everything.'

They sat inside the café, where they'd be undisturbed. All the other customers were outside on the terrace, enjoying the sunshine. Lucie had ordered coffees for them both.

Sitting across from the other woman, she watched as Solange dropped two sugar cubes into her cup, and stirred.

She was about two years older than Lucie, and must have been born shortly after the law came into force, Lucie decided. Back in 1941, she recalled.

Solange put her coffee spoon down.

'Why then? Rebellion!' Her short bark of a laugh held only a trace of humour. 'My adoptive mother didn't like my new boyfriend. So I told her I'd find my real mother and she'd think he was great. Childish, eh?

'The thing was, I'd had a fantastic relationship with my adoptive mother up till that moment. With my dad, too. I knew I was adopted, they'd never made any secret of it, but I also knew they loved me. And I loved them.'

'Same here,' Lucie murmured, her thoughts going to Margot and Ray. 'Except I didn't know I was adopted. That came as a shock.'

Solange shot her a sympathetic look.

'I put the ad in 'Vos Confessions' and a woman answered. She wrote that she had a friend who'd given birth under X here in Angoulême on the twenty-first of August 1942. The day I was born! The woman could be sure of the date, she said, because it was the date of her birthday too.'

'Wow,' Lucie breathed, shocked. 'If it hadn't been her birthday . . . '

'She'd never have remembered the exact date. The difference between finding your birth mother and not finding her is built on coincidences like that, I'm afraid.'

'Sharing the same birthday is something very personal, the sort of thing people would remember,' Lucie said, as much to herself as to the other woman.

'There was a huge explosion that damaged part of the clinic the day I was born. People remember the explosion but not the date it happened.'

Another sympathetic look. Solange paused before continuing.

'This friend became the intermediary between us, and the upshot was, my birth mother and I met in the park round the corner from here.'

Falling silent, she stirred her coffee, slowly, concentrating on the spoon as it went round and round. All at once Lucie sensed the other woman's story was not going to have a happy outcome.

'Don't go on if you'd rather not,' she said, touching her fingers to her own coffee cup. It was cold.

Solange looked up.

'No. I'm here now. I might as well tell you the rest.' She drew in a shaky breath. 'She wasn't married when she had me. Her parents couldn't face the shame, the stigma, of their daughter having a child outside wedlock, so she gave birth to me anonymously — under X — and I was taken away for adoption the very same day.'

She fell silent again. Lucie didn't interrupt.

'She's married now. She's got a husband and three children. I've got two half-sisters and a half-brother, but I'll never get to see any of them.'

Lucie heard the uneasy mix of bitterness and longing in her voice, and reached across the table to give her hand a comforting squeeze.

Solange's mouth twisted.

'She doesn't want her husband or children to find out about me.' She paused for a moment. 'It was obvious she didn't feel anything for me. You could see it in her eyes. A bit of mild curiosity, perhaps, but that was all.'

She dropped two more sugar cubes into her coffee and stirred.

'And, you know, I didn't feel anything for her, either. No empathy. No fellow feeling. No sense of a blood tie. She could have been anyone. I just felt blank. Empty.' She stopped, letting the coffee spoon fall with a clatter into the saucer.

'Oh, Solange.' There was a lump in Lucie's throat. What could she say? How could she ease the other woman's pain?

'And you know what?' Solange's eyes

glittered. 'My adoptive mother was right about my boyfriend. He was a total waster.'

'Are you — have you made it up with her?'

'Yes, of course. She's my mother. The only mother I've ever known.'

The Right Decision?

'I want an honest answer, Yannick.'

Sitting back in his chair, the ankle of one long leg resting on the knee of the other, he slanted a look across the table at her.

'I've never been anything other than truthful with you.' Expression and tone were carefully neutral. Lucie bit her lip.

'I know.' Too truthful, perhaps. Maybe she'd heard one too many unwelcome truths.

It was two days after her meeting with Solange Perron, and she and Yannick had come to a café near Madame Guellerin's house. It had been her idea, but she sensed he was in full agreement. The bench beneath the honeysuckle in her landlady's garden reminded her too cruelly of the time she'd almost — almost? — fallen in love with him.

Like his expression and tone, the

choice of a café was carefully neutral. There was a conversation she needed to have with him, and then he could be on his way, back to his mother's apartment in Tours, or his own in Paris. She didn't care which, she tried to convince herself.

He hadn't come down to Poitiers specially to see her. He'd been investigating a story nearby, he'd told her, a scam being operated by a couple of saffron growers, and intended spending the night in Tours before going to see Réjane d'Aucourte the next morning.

'And?' he prompted. They sat on the terrace. The early evening air was warm and still. Two glasses of wine stood untouched on the table between them.

'Did you put me in touch with Solange Perron because you knew her story would make me think twice?'

'Has it?' The question was softly spoken but his gaze was intent on her face.

'Answer my question, please.'

'Then, no. No, I didn't. As I told you

before, of all the replies I got, she was the only one who'd found her birth mother.' He paused. 'So — has it made you think twice?'

Lucie sighed, taking her time before replying.

'I always knew my birth mother would almost certainly be married and have other — ' her voice faltered over the word ' — children. But what Solange said really brought it home to me. She'll have made a new life for herself. A life that doesn't involve me. She didn't want me then. She might not want me now. Especially if she's told no-one about me.' Her voice trailed to a halt.

When Yannick reached across the table, taking both her hands in his, she didn't pull hers away. She was at a low ebb — the lowest ebb, she realised — and desperately needed his strength, his understanding.

'Don't judge her too harshly, Lucie. She wanted you enough not to choose the alternative.'

For an instant, Lucie could only look

at him blankly. Then understanding came, and with it all the warmth of the day vanished at a stroke. She shuddered.

'You're saying I'm lucky to be alive.' A memory slid into her mind.

'That's what you were going to tell me, back in England, on the beach, wasn't it?' He'd been angry with her, had started to say something but had thought better of it, she remembered.

Yannick nodded.

'That's why the law was passed — to prevent the alternative.'

A back-street abortion. It didn't bear thinking about. She shuddered again, glad for the warmth of his hands round hers.

She looked unhappily at Yannick.

'She must have had a good reason for having me under X — in secret. What if that reason's still valid? If I do ever find her, do I have the right to go bursting in on the life she's built for herself?' She paused, gathering her thoughts. 'Am I doing the right thing, Yannick?'

He didn't answer straight away. He

sat back in his chair, his hands sliding away from hers. His expression, Lucie saw, was carefully neutral once again.

'Are you doing the right thing, Lucie? Only you can answer that.'

* ★ ★

'Lucie. That was well-timed. I've just got in from work.' Yannick's voice, booming and fading by turn down the phone line, held a certain reserve. The memory of that awful row down by the river, followed by the stilted exchanges on the two occasions they'd met since then, were clearly as vivid in his mind as in hers.

'Your mum said to phone around now. I'm at her apartment,' Lucie told him.

'Why? What's wrong? Has something happened to her?'

'No, nothing like that,' Lucie hastened to reassure him. 'She's fine.'

'Then what are you doing in Tours on a Monday?'

Good question. She sat back on the sofa, receiver to her ear. At the other end of the line, she could hear music in the background, an Eddy Mitchell song. Yannick must have turned his radio or record player on when he got back home from the newspaper offices.

'Lucie?'

She sighed.

'I stayed the weekend here with your mum, as usual. I travelled back down to Poitiers last night. And when I woke up this morning, I . . . ' Emotion caught at her voice. ' . . . I just couldn't face another day, another week, of pointless, useless questions. I was getting nowhere. And I never will get anywhere. I accept that now.' Tears had filled her eyes. 'It's over. My search for my mother is over.'

A brief pause, then Yannick spoke.

'Lucie, my sweet. I'm so sorry.' His tone was soft, achingly sincere. There was another pause. 'I wish I could be there with you,' he added.

'So do I,' she said quietly. No recriminations, she noted. No 'I told you so'.

But then she'd never expected him to come out with that kind of thing. 'Will you be able to come down soon?'

'Oh Lucie . . . ' he said, and she sensed an unwillingness to be the cause of further pain. 'I'm snowed under at the moment — things to finish before my holiday begins. I'm interviewing Réjane d'Aucourte on Friday, that's the earliest this coming week I'll be able to get down your way. I'm sorry.'

'No, don't be sorry. That's fine.' She blinked away a tear. 'I'm staying here all week.'

'So phone, or I'll phone you, each evening. And Lucie . . . ' There was a sombre note in his voice. 'You've made the right decision.'

Out of the Blue

Friday afternoon, and Lucie stood at the open window of Arlette's flat, fore-arms on the sill, looking out for Yannick. She was smiling, eager to see him again, and her fingernails drummed an impatient, restless rhythm. It was as if that dreadful row had never happened.

He'd phoned her, or she'd phoned him every evening that week. It was a welcome plus to staying in his mother's flat. Madame Guellerin hadn't been on the phone, of course, and it would have cost Lucie a fortune to phone from a café or the post office time after time.

They'd had long chats about anything and everything — everything except her decision to stop looking for her birth mother. That was something to be talked about face to face, she knew.

The smell of coffee roasting some-where nearby, bread being baked, and food being cooked mingled with the odour of diesel and petrol, all drifting upward through the summer air.

From outside, too, came the unmistakably French sound of car horns blaring. Four o'clock on a Friday afternoon in July and the road below was clogged with car drivers on their way home from work, growing impatient with, or jealous of, the caravans and cars with overloaded roof racks heading south and west to their holiday destinations.

And there he was, crossing the square below, dodging cars, mopeds and cyclists, weaving a path between café tables.

'Yannick!'

With a laugh she ran out of the flat, down the two flights of stairs, out of the main door and on to the pavement. He was only metres away, and saw her immediately.

For the space of a heartbeat he hesitated, as though unsure of his reception. Then his arms came round her, lifting her up, swinging her round. And they were kissing each other, kissing and laughing with the sheer joy of it, oblivious to the people all around.

At last he set her down.

'Whoa, there's a welcome fit for a king.' He touched a finger to her chin. His expression was serious as he scanned her face. 'OK?'

She nodded.

Emotion of a different sort softened his features. His eyes never left hers as he brought his hand up, fingertips brushing a strand of her hair back from her face, before trailing across her cheek, coming to rest on her lower lip.

'Where's Mum?' His voice was low, almost a whisper.

'Out shopping.' Her skin was singing with his touch.

'Probably not a good idea to go up to the apartment, then. I'm not sure I'll be able to keep my hands off you.'

'No.'

'So let's walk, and you can tell me all about it.'

He put his arm round her, pulling her against the strong, lean line of his body, and Lucie's pulses raced as, arm in arm, they headed towards the river.

'Nothing I did ever got me anywhere,' she said after they'd walked a while in a comfortable silence. She shook her head at the memory of those wasted weeks.

'The people in town halls — mostly very nice — they couldn't help me. Adoption agencies — very nice people, but couldn't help me. Doctors — I've been to all the doctors in Poitiers, they couldn't help.

'Friends of Margot and her first husband couldn't help. It's as if I've been banging my head against a brick wall. And nothing I can do can bring that wall down.'

It seemed far more than seven weeks that she'd been in France. She felt she'd been asking questions for ever. Dispiritingly, her research never led to anything. She always came to a dead end.

Her car had been a godsend, enabling

her to travel quickly and easily from one place to another and to return to Tours each weekend where she could recharge her batteries on her aunt's cooking and company in preparation for another tussle with those in authority.

The weekends Yannick had been able to join her there had been a wonderful bonus, of course.

Adoption agencies hadn't been able to help her, as there were questions of confidentiality to be considered.

She'd asked doctors and midwives if they, or anyone they knew, had ever worked at the Clinique du Bon Endroit. Some answered in the affirmative and Lucie had held her breath each time, but none recalled being present at a birth 'under X' on July 29th, 1944.

It was a date some of them remembered because a huge explosion in the nearby railway yard had destroyed part of the clinic.

An air raid in August had damaged the clinic beyond repair. Luckily all the patients had been evacuated in time but a doctor and three nursing staff had regrettably been killed. Had one of those four helped deliver her, Lucie couldn't help wondering.

She was silent. Poor Yannick, she thought. He'd heard all this — had listened patiently — so many times before.

He came to a halt, his hand at her waist turning her to face him, the other coming up to tangle in her hair, drawing her to him.

'So your search for your mother is — over?' He spoke quietly, his expression full of concern. Once again, Lucie had an uncomfortable insight into the impact her futile quest had had on those she loved.

'Yes. Yes, it is.' Her anger, her bitterness, her frustration were all spent. Only resignation was left. The system was there to protect the mother. It was unassailable, she couldn't fight it any more. 'I've put an ad in 'Vos Confessions' and two other magazines. I don't expect to hear anything, though,' she said.

'And I've had a phone call from a man called David Lucas. He works for a film company, Fournier Films . . .'

'Fournier?'

'Yes. Have you heard of them?'

He shook his head, frowning.

'It's a common enough name, I suppose.'

'They're making a film about children born 'under X', and he'd like to interview me.'

The phone call had come out of the blue the Tuesday before.

'Mademoiselle Curtis? My name is David Lucas.' It was a man's voice, quiet and cultured although he mangled the pronunciation of her surname — as, to be fair, did most of the French people Lucie had come across.

'I'm doing research for a film my company is thinking of making about children born to an anonymous mother. An employee at Poitiers town hall gave me your name and phone number.'

'Oh. Yes.' Her mind flew back to the

142

woman, her hair pulled back in a loose old-fashioned bun, who had wanted so much to be helpful. 'Yes, I remember her. Well, ask away.'

There was a pause.

'I would prefer it if we could meet, mademoiselle — to see if you'd be suitable for inclusion in the film. It's a very visual medium, of course.'

Unease had stirred, coming in whispers across her skin. After her experiences of the last few weeks, she was more than happy to help out with anything that would air the plight of children born to a mother who was, and would for ever remain, anonymous. And appearing in a film held no worries for her.

But Monsieur Lucas's wish to meet her in person made her wary. The only reason she agreed to meet him was the possibility, however faint, that he might be able to help her in her search, and caution had governed her choice of a public place in the middle of the day for the meeting, and on a day when she was almost certain Yannick could be there with her — just in case.

She twisted round to look at Yannick now, reached up to touch a kiss to his lips.

'Eleven o'clock tomorrow at the Cheval Blanc. Will you come with me?'

'No need to ask. Of course I will,' he said, kissing her back.

Strange Encounter

'What's the betting that's him?' Lucie leaned her head closer to Yannick's and spoke in an undertone. Sitting next to him on the terrace of one of the cafés in Place Plumereau, his arm warm and heavy across her shoulders, she watched as a man in his 40s made his way towards a young woman sitting alone at a nearby table.

In a dark, narrow-cut two-piece suit, and carrying a briefcase, he looked every inch the businessman. Lucie was surprised. For some reason she hadn't expected him to be so formally dressed.

Yannick, with his shirt open at the neck, its sleeves rolled up, and trousers held at the hips by a belt, looked beautifully casual by comparison, she thought with a smile, loving the way he looked, loving everything about him.

The man must have heard her for he

looked her way. He seemed to do a double-take, and there was something like surprise or shock in the look he sent her.

Lucie caught the frown that followed, the narrowing of his eyes, the glance at Yannick — all in the space of a second — before he switched direction. He'd been expecting her to be by herself, of course, she realised.

'This is your show, Lucie, my sweet,' Yannick said into her ear, his arm sliding from her shoulders as he scraped his metal chair across the cobbles and got to his feet. 'But I'm here if you need me.'

'Mademoiselle Curtis? David Lucas from Fournier Films.' He held out his hand.

Lucie stood and they shook hands across the table.

'Pleased to meet you, Monsieur Lucas. May I introduce my friend, Yannick Savaton? I wanted him to come and meet you, too.'

'Of course. I quite understand.' More handshakes, and she and Yannick sat back down again, while David Lucas slipped his jacket off and hung it carefully over the back of his chair before he too sat, taking a pen and a leather-bound notebook out of his case.

His fashionably slim tie was the exact shade of green as the stripe in his shirt. Gold cufflinks, discreet rather than flashy, held his shirtsleeves at the wrists.

'I couldn't find your company in any phone book, Monsieur Lucas.' Lucie's tone was one of mild enquiry. Nevertheless, she wanted an answer. The morning after his phone call she'd phoned the employee at Poitiers town hall who had confirmed that she had indeed given out Lucie's name and phone number.

'It was to a woman, though,' she'd said, 'not a man. They must work for the same company, don't you think?'

Next, Lucie had gone to the main post office and looked in all the Paris phone books as well as the ones for Poitiers and Tours and their surrounding areas. The name 'Fournier Films' had not been there.

'Well . . . ' He pulled at the knot of his tie, loosening it the barest fraction. 'We're a very new company. We've only been going three months. A new, young company,' he went on, plainly warming to his theme, 'bursting with ideas.' He seemed relieved when the waiter arrived at their table.

The waiter put the parasol up, shielding the three of them from the bright morning sun that now shone down from above the rooftops, and went off with their orders.

Yannick leaned forward.

'What projects are you working on at the moment, monsieur?'

David Lucas gave a little laugh.

'I thought I'd be the one asking you questions.' He paused to consider. 'Well, we specialise in documentaries, as I believe I mentioned over the phone. We've done one about French winegrowers securing a deal in England.

'Another . . . ' He gestured with his arm, taking in the square behind him

148

' . . . about the centre of Tours here, how they're restoring the old buildings, in preference to pulling them down and putting up concrete blocks of flats.

'And of course, one about children born to mothers who wish to remain anonymous, very much in its early days still.'

The waiter arrived with two coffees, and a mineral water for David Lucas. Lucie took advantage of the interruption to dart a look at Yannick. He was leaning back in his chair again, ankle of one leg resting on the knee of the other. He frowned at her and shrugged.

He, too, had clearly picked up on David Lucas' hesitations, but his shrug reassured her and she took it as a signal that he saw no harm in continuing the meeting.

She turned back to David Lucas.

'An interesting mix, monsieur.'

'We like to think so.' He opened the notepad on the table, and took the top off his fountain pen. Lucie saw the name Lucie Curtis printed in capitals at the top of the page. 'Would you mind if I took down some details?'

'Of course not. That's what we're here for.' She tried her coffee. It was hot and strong, very good.

'Your first name is Lucie. Is that the name on your official records?'

'No, it isn't actually. I was given the names Mélusine Jeanne France.'

His hand, poised to write, didn't move. He looked up, and again his gaze moved over her face as if committing her features to memory.

'An unusual first name.'

Lucie gave a rueful smile. The memory was distant now, and no longer hurt.

'The kids at school gave me a hard time over it. That's why I changed it to Lucie.'

'Date of birth?' David Lucas asked, returning his attention to his notepad and writing her name.

'The twenty-ninth of July, 1944. I was probably born in Poitiers, though I can't be a hundred per cent sure.' Lucie watched as he jotted the information down, and thought how terrifying the explosion that ripped through the railway yard must have been for her birth mother.

'I've already got your address and phone number.' He looked up at her and took a sip of his mineral water. 'You live very near here, don't you?'

'It's my aunt's address, actually. Her apartment's just over there.' Lucie pointed behind him to the irregular terrace of tall thin mediaeval houses on the other side of the square. Squeezed together and with overhanging storeys to make the most of the available space, they'd now been divided up into flats.

'Who knows,' she added, 'she might feature in your documentary about the centre of Tours.'

A blank look, so fleeting Lucie thought she must have imagined it.

'Oh, yes.' He smiled. 'My colleagues would know more about that than I do. Tell me,' he went on, 'what do you know, or what have you learned, about the mother you're looking for?'

All at once it was difficult to speak.

'Nothing. I don't know anything.' She thought she'd gone past anger and bitterness, bewilderment and pain, into a zone of numb resignation, but she'd been wrong. It hurt as much now as it ever had. His question had brought it all to the surface again. Her hand went out to her side, seeking Yannick's.

'I'm sorry,' she said to David Lucas, forcing a smile. 'It still gets to me.'

'I can see that,' he said, and there was genuine sympathy in his voice, she thought.

'Look,' he went on, closing his notepad, putting the cap back on his pen and putting both in his case, 'I think we could call it a day for now. I've got your phone number if I need to contact you again. What do you think?'

'Yes. Good idea.' She got to her feet, bringing Yannick up with her.

David Lucas stood too. Putting his jacket back on, he pulled his wallet out of his inside pocket and took a 50 franc note out.

'That should cover it,' he said, placing the note on the table for the waiter before shaking hands with Lucie and Yannick and picking up his briefcase.

The two of them stood side by side as they watched him go. Lucie put her arms round Yannick's waist, hugging him to her. He was heading back to Paris that afternoon and she didn't want him to go.

'What do you think?' she asked, frowning.

'Strange. Just to listen to him — he sounded at times as if he was making the answers up as he went along.'

'I agree.' Lucie's frown deepened. David Lucas had crossed the square and was getting into a dusty Citroën DS. Her mind went over those hesitations of his, the curious way he'd looked at her at times, his wanting to meet her in person. And he'd asked far too few questions, surely.

'Maybe he decided early on that my story wasn't right for his film,' Lucie

said, shaking her head. 'The whole
thing was a bit weird, though, wasn't it?
Off-key.'

Breathtaking Proposal

The following Saturday, July 29, was Lucie's birthday. She'd spent the week at Viviane Guellerin's house in Poitiers, and now her landlady placed on the table creamy unsalted butter, a jar of her homemade apricot jam and croissants, fresh and flaky, still warm from the bakery.

'This is so delicious,' Lucie said, dunking one end of her croissant into the cup the size of a soup bowl that held her coffee.

Viviane laughed, clearly relishing her enjoyment. Reaching behind her, she brought up a parcel that she handed to Lucie.

'Happy birthday, Lucie, *ma chère*. This was my daughter's when she was your age.' Her daughter, Lucie knew, had died in the war. 'I'd like you to have it.'

It was a flower press, with an album to put the pressed flowers in, and Lucie was deeply moved. The first pages of the album contained purple pansies and passion flowers, and roses of all colours still carrying a lingering trace of their fragrance, and she made a mental vow to fill the remaining pages.

'Thank you, Viviane,' she said. 'I'll treasure it always.'

The postman brought cards from friends in England, plus a card from her stepfather and one from her agent who'd added a PS at the end of her message: 'See you on August 28th.'

In less than a month, Lucie thought with a pang, she'd be back in England, and her mind seemed suddenly numb as though it didn't know how to react to that notion.

By mid-morning she was heading up the main road to Tours for lunch followed by a tour of the shops and galleries with Arlette.

As she drove north, she was conscious of a growing excitement fizzing through her veins — she'd soon be seeing Yannick again.

He'd left Tours shortly after their meeting with David Lucas, saying with a frown he intended doing further checks on Fournier Films, and had been in Paris all week.

Cost and inconvenience meant she hadn't been able to phone him. She'd missed him terribly, she realised. She'd filled her days exploring Poitiers and its surrounding area, but it was Yannick who filled her mind.

She couldn't stop thinking about him, wondering where he was, what he was doing, and she longed to be with him again, to feel his warm strong arms around her, to smell the lemony scent of his aftershave and the salt tang of his skin.

Soon. She'd be with him again soon.

She gave a long happy sigh as she and her aunt walked back, arms linked, to Arlette's apartment several hours later.

'I reckon I'll have put on a kilo or

two by the end of the day.' They'd eaten moules marinières at a little restaurant near the covered market.

'Nonsense,' Arlette said with a laugh. 'Mussels are very healthy. And we've done a lot of walking.'

'Don't forget there's the birthday meal this evening, too.'

Lucie frowned. There was something familiar about the man who stood with his back to them close to the main entrance to the apartments where Arlette lived.

He wore a blue and white checked shirt, and grey trousers. A tendril of smoke curled up into the air above him.

The man turned, taking the pipe from his mouth, and a smile beamed across her face.

'Dad!'

He saw her at the same moment, held his arms out and she was racing towards him, just as she had so many times throughout her childhood.

'I thought I'd surprise the birthday girl.'

'You did. You did. A lovely surprise,' she said, breathing in the familiar smells of tobacco and soap.

Arlette joined them, and he half-released her in order to draw his sister-in-law into a hug. One look at her aunt's face told Lucie that Ray's arrival hadn't come out of the blue.

'You're a pair of rotters,' Lucie accused, laughing. 'You could have told me.'

'Then it wouldn't have been a surprise,' her stepfather rejoined with impeccable logic.

'You even sent me a card to put me off the scent. Don't look so smug!'

They were upstairs in Arlette's apartment and had just sat down to have their coffee when Yannick arrived from Paris. The door swung open, he put his suitcase down just inside and stood in the doorway brandishing two bottles of pétillant, one in each hand.

The breath caught in Lucie's throat as she took in his dark hair, those arching eyebrows above eyes that sparkled with *joie de vivre*, his smiling mouth, and the strong line of his jaw. He looked magnificent.

Arlette's eyebrows went up.

'Two bottles?' she asked, getting to her feet.

'A double celebration. Lucie's birthday, and the start of my holiday.'

He came into the apartment and set the bottles on the coffee table before wrapping his mother, then his uncle, in a warm hug. No surprise to see Ray, Lucie noted. It was clear Yannick had been in on the secret, too.

Finally he stood before her. Their eyes met as he bent towards her, and the brief touch of his lips on hers was like a caress, whispering across her skin.

'You look happy,' she said quietly.

'I am. Four weeks' holiday,' he said, smiling. 'And . . . ' He started to say more, but turned to his uncle instead. 'Good to see you again, Ray, even if it's only a flying visit.'

'That's right. I'll be leaving tomorrow, just before lunch. I'm going on to some friends down near the Med but

I'll be back here for a few days in August some time.'

Lucie moved over to him, wrapping both arms round one of his.

'Good. I'm glad.'

Preparing the birthday meal was a joint effort — all four of them played their part — and was accompanied by lots of laughter and fun. At last everything was ready: glasses and best china gleamed on the damask tablecloth, and the smell of rich food cooking, tempting the taste buds, drifted in from the kitchen.

The four of them took their places, and Yannick opened the bottle of pétillant, filling long-stemmed glasses with the foaming wine, pushing a glass across the table to each of them in turn.

'To Lucie,' he said, raising his glass. 'Happy birthday, and many happy returns.'

'Thank you.' As she looked at the happy, smiling faces of the three people with her, her heart was filled with warmth.

Yes, a woman somewhere had given

birth to her 24 years before, but this was her family, this was where she belonged.

The food was delicious. Smoked salmon with chives and crème fraiche was followed by chicken that had been simmering in red wine for several hours, served with creamy dauphinoise potatoes.

Then came salad and a selection of tangy cheeses. And to finish, the dessert, one of the local pâtissier's special strawberry tarts, but decorated, English-style, with 24 candles.

'Oh no!' Lucie laughed when Arlette struck a match and held it to the first of them. 'I've been laughing so much I haven't got any puff left.'

It had been that sort of meal. They'd spoken about all kinds of subjects, from the lightest to the most serious, discussing, simply chatting, arguing at times, above all, laughing.

Lucie had always loved the French tradition of celebrating a birthday or an important family event with a meal, and this had been one of the best.

Her thoughts went to Margot, who had so enjoyed catering for events like this — how Lucie wished she were still here with her. She sighed and smiled at the same time, and wasn't surprised when Yannick covered her hand with his, giving it a little squeeze.

'Thinking of Margot?' He mouthed the words. She nodded, moved that he'd read her mind so well.

The candles were blown out, the tart eaten, the last of the wine drunk.

'Ray and I will clear this lot away,' Arlette said.

Yannick took Lucie's hand in his.

'Come outside. We'll walk a while.'

It was almost midnight, but the air was still warm with the summer's heat. They walked only a few metres, strolling hand in hand, before Yannick turned to face her, catching her hands in each of his.

'Have you enjoyed your birthday?' he asked softly.

The moon, a half-moon high in the

sky, highlighted the strong lines of his face, and she was only too aware how much she wanted to kiss him.

'You know I have,' she replied, equally softly.

'You're very special to me, Lucie. Very special.' He released one of her hands, his hand coming up to her face, and the pad of his thumb traced a slow line, following the curve of her lower lip. 'Will you marry me, Lucie?'

For a long moment she couldn't speak. His words had taken the breath from her lungs. She looked into his eyes, conscious of the rapid beat of her heart, barely heard the footsteps on the pavement, the muted voices of people going home for the night.

With a hand that shook slightly, she reached up, touching her fingertips to his jaw, rough with the very masculine rasp of the next day's beard.

'Yes, Yannick. Yes, I will.'

And with a sound low in his throat, he gathered her to him, drawing her hard against the lean length of his body.

His mouth came down on hers, and she gave herself over to the exquisite beauty of his kiss.

Bitter Truth

So that was what the second bottle of bubbly was for, Lucie thought, beaming with happiness as she and Yannick let themselves into his mother's flat.

Ray and Arlette had cleared everything away and were now sitting opposite each other, playing a game of cards. There was something expectant about the way both of them looked at Yannick that told Lucie they'd known what he was going to do. But she didn't mind. She didn't mind at all. She was the happiest woman in the world.

The advertisement she'd put in three magazines yielded nothing apart from a reply from a clairvoyant offering to read her mother's identity in the tarot cards. And David Lucas didn't phone back, but Lucie had never really expected him to.

As the long summer days went by,

July slipping effortlessly into August, she pushed the memory of that odd interview — if interview was the right word — to the back of her mind, and gave herself over to the sheer enjoyment of spending her time with the man she loved.

In the comparative cool of the morning, they walked hand in hand through woods and along the banks of rivers. In the heat of the day they visited châteaux and museums.

In the evenings they sampled a range of French theatre, from the classical elegance of Racine's 'Phèdre' at the opera house in Tours to a low-budget rough-round-the-edges production of Beckett's 'Waiting for Godot' in a village hall in the middle of nowhere.

And at night, she went back to Madame Guellerin's or to Arlette's flat, while Yannick stayed in a nearby hotel, as he'd done in fact on the night of her birthday.

'You mean the world to me, Lucie,' he'd said. 'We're going to do things properly. Our first night together will be in the honeymoon suite of a luxury château somewhere.'

'I'm not sure how long we're going to be able to stick to that resolution,' she said, wrapping her arms round his neck.

'Nor am I.' He laughed, and he bent to give her one of those long, lingering kisses that she loved so much.

Gradually she came to terms with her failure to find the woman who had given birth to her. She'd got nowhere. It had been French bureaucracy at its worst, an iron curtain more rigid and inflexible than the one that separated East from West Germany.

Little by little the hurt, the anger, the frustration of her wasted weeks in France subsided, didn't fill her mind so completely.

With Yannick at her side, she managed to think more and more of other things.

It was Assumption, August 15, the day when French people start to think about going back to work or school after the lazy days of summer.

She and Yannick had to set a date for the wedding. Would they live in England or France? They hadn't decided yet. And in a little under two weeks, she'd be starting rehearsals for her part in the new soap.

Excitement tempered by a certain apprehension fizzed inside her, made her light-headed — a whole new chapter of her life was about to begin.

It was Arlette who suggested they spend the day in 'Mélusine Country', as she put it.

'It's an area south-west of Poitiers. About an hour's drive away. Here, take this,' she said, handing Lucie a leaflet. 'It tells you the places to go to and the things you can see there.'

So they'd driven south down the RN10 in search of Lucie's namesake. Still somewhat surprised that she hadn't thought of the idea herself, Lucie wound the car window down, letting the wind stream through her hair and the glorious sunshine play on her skin.

Turning in the seat, a smile on her lips, she watched Yannick's fine-boned hands on the wheel, studied his beautiful profile, loved it when he reached across to catch her hand in his.

Near Coulombiers, hand in hand, they walked through the wood where Mélusine first met the man she'd marry, Lord Raymondin.

They sipped fragrant coffee in Lusignan, in a café close to the ruins of the castle Raymondin could only have built with Mélusine's magic to help him.

After lunch in a village a few kilometres away, they walked round the church where Mélusine had brought her eight sons, one by one, each touched in some way by the fairy mark, for Christian baptism.

There was a carving of her, on the outside of the church, high above the arched doorway. It showed her, long hair curling over her breasts, comb in one hand and mirror in the other, her woman's body transformed into a serpent's tail from the waist down as she took her Saturday bath.

Lucie stood beside Yannick, looking up at the carving, before turning away, oddly dissatisfied as she headed back to the car.

They now stood side by side, looking up at another carving, this time on the tower Mélusine was said to have thrown up overnight, built on the crest of a small hill far from any town or village.

Even so, it was a popular site. There were several cars in the car park and two others had arrived at the same time as she and Yannick.

The happy shouts of children as they raced round the circular tower filled the air. In ones and twos, people went up to the door and looked in. Some ventured up the stone steps inside the building. Fewer still came round to this, the sheltered, shady side of the tower.

The carving had been cut into a large slab of limestone set into the wall. Though facing east, away from the wind and the rain, the weather had blunted its sharp edges over the centuries.

It showed a Mélusine with many-pointed dragon's wings rising up from her back, dipping forward above her to make a protective arc. Her arms too came out in a circle that didn't meet, as though inviting people into her embrace. Gone was the vanity and self-centredness that had struck Lucie so negatively in the other carving.

She turned to look at Yannick, a smile on her face.

'This is much better. I feel an affinity with this Mélusine.'

A middle-aged man, stepping past her as he made his way to the wall of the tower, checked for an instant and gave her a look. She and Yannick had been speaking English, she realised. They were quite far from the obvious tourist sites and English voices probably weren't very common here, she thought.

He carried a posy of wildflowers, and she watched with idle curiosity as he laid them at the foot of the wall beneath the carving.

There was a sadness in the action

and in the way that he stepped back a couple of paces and simply stood there, head bowed, that touched her deeply. She looked up at Yannick and knew that he'd seen it too when he put his arm round her, drawing her to him.

The man turned and saw them watching him. His mouth sketched a smile, though his eyes behind thick glasses glittered.

'It's her birthday today,' he said. He spoke in English, and added in explanation, 'I heard you just now. I teach English, in a college near here.' He looked away, up to the carving on the wall, and back to the posy on the ground. 'I always come up here on my Mélusine's birthday.'

There was silence. Lucie was lost for words. His sadness was palpable. Yannick, at her side, shifted his stance, his hand tightening round her arm.

'Your Mélusine?' she asked at last, quietly, some instinct putting her on full alert. All at once she hardly dared breathe.

'That was her codename, of course.'

He gave a short, jerky sigh. 'No. Not my Mélusine. Never mine. She only had eyes for . . . ' He broke off, mouth twisting, and he turned, aiming spittle at the grass behind him.

Lucie almost jumped, shocked to the core by the depth of anger and disgust the gesture revealed.

The man pulled a handkerchief out of his jacket pocket, blew his nose, wiped his mouth, and looked at her, blinking rapidly, as if he were seeing her for the first time.

'You look like her, you know. You've got her height and build too.' He glanced down at the posy of flowers. 'I lost touch with her. Way back then. She disappeared for several months. I was distraught.'

'Disappeared? For several months?' She spoke the words softly and felt Yannick stiffen, his hand slowly stroking her arm. She couldn't move. The children's voices faded into the distance.

This couldn't be happening. She didn't believe it. All those weeks — and now, a chance encounter was giving her the answer. It couldn't be true.

She felt she was standing, finely balanced, on the edge of a precipice. Did she have the courage to take the next step?

She opened her mouth to speak. Her mouth was too dry. She swallowed.

'When?' Her voice was husky. 'When did she disappear? And why?'

He shook his head.

'I've no idea. But she came back about the time this area was liberated. September 1944. Why do you want to know?'

She swallowed again, gathering strength from Yannick who stood behind her now, both hands firm, supportive, on her arms.

'No reason,' she said, shaking her head. She couldn't take it in. Was it possible she'd found her mother? She wanted to jump and leap and dance, soar through the air, and share her joy with the whole world.

'Tell me, monsieur . . . ' she began.

'Lemercier. François Lemercier.'

'Tell me about your Mélusine,

Monsieur Lemercier,' Lucie said. 'Is she still alive? Did she and — um, whoever — get married? Where does she live?' The questions kept spilling out, she couldn't stop them, couldn't stop the happiness that bubbled through her. At last! She'd found her at last. She still couldn't believe it.

François Lemercier took his glasses off, started polishing them with his handkerchief.

'Yes, she's still alive. Very much so.' His voice was low, heavy with sadness for the woman he still loved, Lucie sensed.

'Even if you've only been here a week or so, you'll have seen pictures of her. She's the one they're calling the French Jackie Kennedy. Réjane d'Aucourte.' He put his glasses back on and gave Lucie a bleak smile. 'Though when I knew her, she was still Réjane Fournier, of course.'

The Cruellest Blow

'Fournier?' It was as though Lucie had been punched in the stomach, the air pushed from her lungs. It was the cruellest blow imaginable. She must have cried out, some shocking sound that stopped the running children in their tracks.

Yannick was turning her round, wrapping her in his arms, pulling her head down on to his shoulder, stroking her hair as juddering sobs tore through her.

Fournier. Fournier Films. It had been her mother who had contacted the town hall in Poitiers, Lucie was sure of it. She'd sent David Lucas to — what? Look her over? Find out more? And then? Nothing. It was a bitter truth. Three weeks of nothing.

The gut-wrenching pain of it was beyond endurance. Her mother had rejected her at birth — and again three weeks ago. Lucie had been abandoned by her own mother, not once, but twice.

But there was worse.

'You knew!' She faced Yannick, chest heaving. 'You knew her maiden name was Fournier.' No need to explain who 'she' was. 'You must have done. You always do your research. When you first heard the name — Fournier Films — you must have made the connection.' She gulped in a breath. 'Why didn't you tell me?'

His face was pale, all colour drained from it.

'There are hundreds — thousands — of Fourniers in France. It's one of the commonest surnames there is. The chances of Fournier Films and Réjane d'Aucourte being connected were slim to say the least.'

'That was your judgement.' She flung the words at him. 'And it was wrong.'

She glanced up at the carving of Mélusine, across at the posy of flowers. François Lemercier had gone. She hadn't seen him go.

She looked at Yannick and felt her

heart was breaking.

'You said you were going to do further checks on Fournier Films. Did you? Or was that a promise you had no intention of keeping?' She saw him flinch, head jolting back as though she'd dealt him a punch. 'You certainly never told me what you found out.'

'There was nothing to find out.' Anger equal to her own pulsed from him. 'I drew a blank. A total blank. I decided it was some kind of con. You hadn't come to any harm, so I let it go.'

'You've been against me finding her from the very start.'

'Against you, no! I said it was impossible. There's a difference.'

'But it wasn't was it? It wasn't impossible. I've found her.'

She saw him suck in a breath and pause before speaking.

'You haven't found her yet, Lucie. It might not be her. Although, yes, it does seem possible Réjane d'Aucourte is your mother.'

Her mouth worked with the emotion

of it. Her mother. At last.

'Lucie, don't do this to yourself.' He reached out, catching one of her hands in his, drawing her to him. Gently, he pushed her head down against his shoulder, stroked her hair, made soothing noises in her ear.

She expelled a shaky breath. Wrapped in his strong arms, held against the warmth of his body, it was so easy to be soothed. She knew she'd been unfair. Whatever he'd done, or not done, had been to protect her, to keep her from harm. She knew that. But still . . .

She lifted her head, pulled away, conscious of her loss as his arms fell to his sides. She looked into his eyes, saw concern for her. Her chin came up.

'I don't want us to see each other any more, Yannick. Not until I — until I know more.' Her voice shook. Tears were wet on her cheeks. She cuffed them away. She wouldn't cry.

'Until you know more.' His tone was low, and dangerous. She heard anger and something else — anguish? — in his voice. 'And after that?'

For a long moment, she couldn't speak. The murmur of voices, the yells of children, the call of rooks — all were muted, coming at her as if from a great distance.

'After that? I don't know.' She swung away. 'Take me back to my digs, please.'

They walked down the hill to the car and drove back to Poitiers in silence. When Yannick pulled up outside Viviane Guellerin's house, she turned to look at him.

'I've got a favour to ask you, Yannick. You knew she had a secret. It seems likely I'm the secret she was hiding. So what I'm asking is, will you promise not to mention it in any further article you may write about her?'

She saw him stiffen as she spoke.

'If you need to ask . . . ' He bit the words out. 'If you think my ethical standards are so low I'd quite happily make money out of your distress, then maybe it's just as well we won't be seeing each other any more.'

Lucie opened her mouth to protest, closed it again. It was over, she realised as she got out of the car.

Their relationship was over.

Brave Decision

'You've got to phone her. You really must my dear.' Lucie's stepfather sat down in the armchair next to hers and leaned forward, elbows on knees, the bowl of his pipe held cupped in the palms of his hands. 'You'll kick yourself for ever if you don't.'

'I agree.' Arlette poured coffee into one of those tall handle-less cups Lucie always found so strange, and pushed it across the low table to her niece.

The phone sat, a squat, menacing presence, in the middle of the table, its flex trailing across the tiles to the socket in the wall.

It was eleven o'clock the morning after her encounter with François Lemercier and her break-up with Yannick, and the three of them were in the living-room of Arlette's apartment.

Her stepfather's arrival at Madame

Guellerin's house the evening before had been the one bright spot in what had turned into a horrendous day.

That morning they'd travelled in convoy up to Tours. They'd both stay at Arlette's for a few days before Ray carried on to the ferry port while Lucie returned to Poitiers.

'Yannick says it's over between the two of you,' Arlette had said when Lucie and Ray arrived at her apartment. There was great sadness in her eyes.

'Yes. It is.' Lucie felt numb. She'd cried herself to sleep the night before, and knew her face was blotchy, her eyes red-rimmed.

'He's gone on to Paris,' Arlette had added. 'He won't be back for a while.'

With a shake of her head, Lucie brought her thoughts back to the present. François Lemercier had said the woman who was — possibly — her mother had had the codename 'Mélusine'. That argued she'd been part of the Resistance during the war.

With a shudder, Lucie recalled the

way he'd spat at the thought of the man she'd fallen in love with. Why? Because he was jealous? Or was there some other reason?

'Shall I phone her? I don't know. I just don't know.' Normally so decisive, she was in an agony of indecision. Could she risk a third rejection?

Putting her coffee down, she stood up, moved restlessly over to the window and looked outside. What should she do for the best?

She could see the café, the bright parasols, the table where she'd sat with Yannick for that off-key meeting with David Lucas. She shut her eyes against the sight. She didn't want any reminder of moments she'd shared with Yannick.

But there were reminders of him everywhere. She could smell lingering, tantalising traces of his aftershave in the apartment.

Lucie opened her eyes, looked out without seeing anything. The last 20 or so hours should have been some of the happiest in her life. She'd achieved the impossible — she'd found her mother. Probably, she cautioned herself. Possibly, she amended. She mustn't get her hopes up too high.

Maybe she'd somehow got things horribly wrong. Leaped to a conclusion that should never have been drawn.

Perhaps there was no connection between the name she'd been given at birth and the woman who'd had the codename Mélusine. No connection either between the woman whose maiden name was Fournier and an elusive film company called Fournier Films making a documentary about children born 'under X'.

Pure coincidence? Or solid clues?

And did it mean that Réjane d'Aucourte, formerly Réjane Fournier, was her mother, but that, when her emissary David Lucas reported back, she decided — for, no doubt, perfectly understandable reasons — that she didn't want even to meet her daughter?

Heavens, how it hurt! Lucie swung away from the window, slamming her hand across her mouth. Rejected as a baby, and again as an adult, sight unseen. The cruelty of it was crippling.

'Lucie, my dear.' Her stepfather had come over to the window, now put his arm round her shoulder, drawing her to him. He smelled of tobacco, the same reassuringly familiar brand he'd smoked since her early childhood, and the pain eased a little. 'What I find odd,' he said, 'is this person who contacted Poitiers town hall, the one making a film. I don't see how she could possibly be your mother.'

'But . . .'

'No, hear me out,' he said, not unkindly. 'If she was your mother, why would she phone the town hall? The system guarantees her anonymity — as you've found out all too well — so if she doesn't want to be found, all she has to do is keep quiet.'

Lucie sighed, unconvinced.

'And the coincidence of the name Fournier?' She looked towards her aunt.

'I agree with Ray. The whole thing is odd. You've got to phone her.'

'Yes.' All at once, Lucie's decision was made. She pulled her shoulders back, steeling herself. 'You're right. Both right,' she said, and crossed to the low table, sitting down on the sofa.

About to lift the receiver, she looked up in surprise when her stepfather's hand covered hers.

'Let me make the initial contact,' he said.

'It's OK. I can do it.'

'Chances are, someone else is going to take the call, and they'll put it through to her or go and find her. And when they say 'There's a Miss Curtis on the line, madame,' what do you think's going to happen?'

'She might refuse to take the call.' It shouldn't hurt so much, but it did.

'So I'm going to lie about my name,' he said with the hint of a smile, the first smile Lucie had seen on any of their faces that morning.

She and Arlette watched as Ray dialled the number. They all three heard the ringing tone that sounded so much like the English engaged tone. A woman's voice. Was it — ? No, not her. A secretary or maid, perhaps.

'S-m-i-t-h. R-a-y-m-o-n-d S-m-i — ' He paused, then put his hand over the mouthpiece. 'She said, '*patientez*'.'

Hold the line. Sweat pricked out on Lucie's palms. Not long now, she knew, and stared at the receiver with something like horror when her stepfather passed it to her.

Oh, Yannick. How she wished he were there with her right now.

Slowly, as if in a daze, Lucie held it to her ear. She saw her aunt usher Ray towards the kitchen. The door closed behind the two of them. She was alone with the phone.

At first, nothing. Then she heard the sound of movement, high heels across a wood floor, perhaps, and finally, a voice spoke into the phone.

'Réjane d'Aucourte.'

Lucie couldn't speak. Her mouth was too dry. The voice was warm, assured, cultured in the way that David Lucas's had been. Was it her mother's voice? She hardly dared hope.

She swallowed, cleared her throat.

'Good morning . . . '

'I was told there was a man, an Englishman called Smith, on the phone.' A certain reserve had entered her voice.

'My stepfather. We thought you might not want to speak to me if you knew who I was.'

'Very cryptic. Please explain what you mean, mademoiselle.' Coolly polite. The warmth that had been there had gone, and Lucie shivered.

'My name is Lucie Curtis. But the names on my official papers are Mélusine Jeanne France.' All at once Lucie's heart tipped into a fast, shallow beat. Had she imagined that intake of breath? Or was it simply a whisper of interference on the line?

'I believe you had the codename 'Mélusine' during the war,' she went on.

'Who told you that?' It was the tone of a light, friendly enquiry. But Lucie was conscious of an underlying — what? Unease? If only she could see the other woman's face.

'A man called François Lemercier.' The silence stretched and stretched, so much so that Lucie wondered if Réjane d'Aucourte had put the phone back down. 'Hello? Are you still there, madame?'

'Yes. I must apologise.' Her voice was gruff. 'It was a name from the past. It brought back memories.' Another pause. 'I sense you have a story to tell, mademoiselle.'

'Yes.'

'Give me your number. I'll phone you back.'

Moments later Lucie put the receiver back in its cradle and looked at her hand in astonishment. It was shaking. Her whole body was shaking in a massive release of tension.

She heard the door to the kitchen click open and she rose unsteadily to her feet, watching as Ray and Arlette came towards her, faces both curious and anxious.

'I did it,' she said. 'Let's see what happens next. She said she'd phone back.'

She saw the two of them exchange a cautious look, and understood their concern. A promise to phone back could be seen as little better that an outright rejection.

But she didn't care. It sounded more positive, and she wanted so much to be positive. It helped her forget that Yannick wasn't there to share this moment with her.

So Many Reminders

Lucie's hand shook as she put the phone back in its cradle and looked at her stepfather and aunt.

'She did phone.' There was no need for her to say who 'she' was. Lucie's happy, disbelieving smile told it all. 'She wants to see me tomorrow.'

'Tomorrow? She's not wasting any time.' Ray tilted his head back, blowing a stream of pipe smoke towards the ceiling. 'I'd like to phone Yannick, tell him what you've arranged. If that's all right with you?'

Lucie drew in a shaky breath, then nodded. Yannick wasn't part of her life any more.

'Where are you seeing her?' Ray asked.

'At her home.'

'Not somewhere more neutral?' Arlette murmured, and Lucie felt a faint unease stir.

* * *

'I'll drive you over there tomorrow,' Lucie's stepfather said.

'Then take a book to read, Ray,' Arlette said, ever practical. 'She might be some time.'

The three of them — Lucie, Ray and Arlette — had walked 200 or so metres northward from the flat and had come to the banks of the Loire. The water was choppy and a breeze came off it, a cool contrast to the warmth of the early evening.

She'd walked this way with Yannick, several times. They'd stood beneath that tree, watching the birds swoop low over the river. He'd kissed her there.

Would it always be like this, she wondered, tearing her gaze away from the tree, only to see the baker winding in his awning.

One day during a sudden shower, they'd sheltered beneath that awning and had spent long laughter-filled minutes deciding which of the pastries looked the most delicious. He'd kissed her there, too.

Would it always be like this, she asked herself again. Would every sight, sound, smell, at every turn, remind her of him? With an effort, she brought her thoughts back to the present.

Turning his back on the breeze, Ray held a lit match to the bowl of his pipe and sucked on the stem until the tobacco caught.

'You might not, uh, feel up to driving yourself.'

After her meeting with Réjane d'Aucourte, that was what he meant, Lucie thought with a shiver.

Ray put the hand that wasn't holding his pipe across her shoulders, drawing her close. On her other side, Arlette linked arms with her. She was so lucky, she thought with a pang, to have people who loved her so much.

'I'll have my official papers with me,' she said. 'They'll prove who I am. I'm hoping she'll just look at them and say, yes, she is my mother. I'm sure she is, there are just too many coincidences otherwise, but — well, I might be wrong.'

Ray gave her shoulder a squeeze and pressed a kiss to the top of her head.

'I'm scared,' she said. 'I was looking for a mother. My mother. But it's not just her and me any more. She's a woman with a family. She's got a husband, sons.'

Lucie had gone to the nearest news-agent's and to the library to get hold of all the papers and magazines which contained articles about Réjane d'Aucourte and had spent the day reading up on her.

She already had copies of the three articles Yannick had written about her, of course.

Réjane Fournier, she'd learned, was the only child of Eléonore and Théophile Fournier, and had married Corentin d'Aucourte in 1945. There'd been a photo of the two of them, taken recently, in one of the articles she'd read. A good-looking couple, and they'd looked happy. But then, most people smiled for a photo.

'You could say he was the 'boy next door',' she said. 'The two families had neighbouring estates.'

'Hmm. A love match?' Arlette wondered out loud. 'Or an arranged marriage?'

According to François Lemercier, Lucie recalled, Réjane had been in love with someone. Was Corentin d'Aucourte that someone? Her heart missed a beat. Was he her father?

No. That didn't make sense. If the two of them had been in love and due to marry, why would they have given their baby away? She shook her head, shaking the notion away.

'They've got two boys. The younger one's just turned twenty, the other one's a year older.'

'No doubt both are destined,' Ray said, 'to follow in their father's footsteps. Fournier d'Aucourte bubbly is known all over the world.'

Lucie twisted round to look at him.

'It's good stuff. I've tried it. With Yannick, in London.' Would his name never stop springing into her mind?

'Réjane d'Aucourte,' she said, making an effort to pull herself together, 'is hoping to be elected to parliament.' She'd been chosen as the socialist candidate for the area, and would contest the seat at the by-election in September.

'And they live in a beautiful *manoir* surrounded by vineyards,' she went on. A photo of the *manoir* accompanied one of the articles Yannick had written, its gleaming creamy-white stone a sparkling contrast to the lush green land all around it.

What came through above all in Yannick's articles was admiration. Every tough question he'd thrown at her, Lucie had read, was lobbed straight back at him — and always graciously, with great charm.

She knew her stuff, could quote laws and cite precedents, and was driven by a fierce desire to improve the lot of ordinary people, women in particular.

Lucie heaved in a breath.

'How will I fit in? Will I fit in? Will I even get that opportunity? Will I want to fit in?' Her smile was wan. 'It's all so complicated. I'm beginning to think I shouldn't have contacted her in the first place.'

'But you did. And you couldn't have done anything else,' Arlette said.

'Your aunt's right,' Ray said. 'You can't change things now, Lucie, my dear.' He paused before continuing. 'I hope you get the happy-ever-after ending you want. But I can't help thinking it's not going to be as simple as that.'

* * *

Words spoken in anger. Stupid, stupid, stupid. Not for the first time that day, Yannick sank down heavily on to the sofa in his Paris flat. Elbows on knees, he buried his head in his hands.

God, how he missed her. Already, and it had only been a day. He missed her smile and her laugh. He missed the way, for no reason, she'd reach out and touch her fingertips to his face, tracing the line of his mouth or jaw or eyebrows, and he could see the desire in her eyes as she did so.

And he missed her honesty and romanticism and, yes, her courage, the way she'd ignored the doom merchants in pursuit of her dream.

Doom merchants. And he'd been chief among them of course. With a sound of self-disgust, he stood up, pacing between the sofa and the window. How could it have happened? How had he let it happen?

A quarrel, a simple quarrel, had blown up out of all proportion, and now they'd split up.

It was his fault. There'd been some basis — more than some — in what she'd said, what she'd accused him of. And now it was over.

Tomorrow, she'd be going to the home of the woman who was almost certainly her mother, and he wouldn't be there at her side.

He stood still for a moment, pushing fingers like claws through his hair and started pacing again. He was afraid for her, very afraid. Would Réjane d'Aucourte welcome her long-lost daughter with open arms? Or would she find the presence of an unwanted daughter an acute embarrassment?

The second option, surely. This was the secret she'd been hiding from him, he had no doubt in his mind of that. He understood why she'd want it kept hidden: it could be death to her political career.

Who — what woman, especially — would vote for someone who'd borne a child 'under X' and given it away? And her failure to get in touch with her daughter after the meeting with David Lucas — that too argued the outcome wouldn't be a happy one.

David Lucas — another question with no answer. Did he really work for a film company? Yannick had found no trace of him. Or was he a friend of the d'Aucourtes? An employee, perhaps. Or . . . ? Yannick frowned. David Lucas was in his 40s, about the same age as Réjane. Was he the man she'd been in love with? Lucie's father?

Yannick paced over to the window and looked out. What should he do? What should he do for the best? The sun had vanished behind the high rooftops when he finally came to a decision.

Moving across to his desk, he picked up the phone and dialled the number.

★ ★ ★

Lucie couldn't get to sleep that night. It was warm, and she lay in bed with just a sheet to cover her. The windows were open, letting a small drift of air into the room. Music from one of the cafés in the square below filtered in through the shutters. Laughter, too, and the occasional shout.

What was going to happen tomorrow? What would it be like? Would Réjane d'Aucourte admit that, yes, she was her mother? Did her husband — Corentin — did he know? What if he didn't?

What if Réjane d'Aucourte said that, no, she wasn't her mother?

202

Questions. So many questions. Too many questions, turning endlessly in her mind.

François Lemercier had said she looked like 'his Mélusine', and that was strange because she'd seen photos of Réjane d'Aucourte, and she couldn't see any similarity.

And Yannick had met her, had interviewed her, several times, and he hadn't seen any similarity either. If he had, he would surely have said.

So maybe she wasn't her mother after all.

Or perhaps it took a stranger to see any likeness.

Her thoughts went to Solange Perron. Poor Solange. She'd found her birth mother. She should have been the happiest woman alive. But instead, it had all gone wrong. Her birth mother didn't want to know. She'd made a new life for herself, and it didn't include Solange.

What if Réjane d'Aucourte felt the same way? Was that what she was going to tell her tomorrow? With something like a sob, Lucie twisted on to her other side, pulling the sheet up around her ears.

How she wished Yannick were with her. He'd hold her, stroke her hair, murmur soft words of comfort, ease her fears away.

But he was in Paris, and he'd never hold her like that again.

No Turning Back

A sense of urgency governed Yannick's every action the following morning. He set out early, when the streets of Paris were grey in the dawn light, and mostly empty.

He had to find out. He had to know.

He stopped at a kiosk to get the latest edition of the 'Clairon Hebdomadaire', out that morning, before jumping back into his car and driving off at speed.

The traffic was light. He'd make good going. For the first part of the journey if not the rest.

With a curse he pulled out to avoid a cyclist. This was no good. He had to stop thinking about her. Concentrate on his driving.

He glanced across at the magazine on the passenger seat. No need to flip through the pages till he came to the article he'd written.

He'd helped choose the photo that went with it, a stock photo from the end of the war, not one she'd provided.

It showed three women lined up, stripped down to their under-slips, heads shaved. Minutes after the photo was taken, he knew, the rest of their clothes had been pulled from them, and they'd been forced to walk through the crowd, paraded through the town, jeered at, shamed before everyone: their punishment for sleeping with the enemy.

It made a great story, Yannick knew. Réjane d'Aucourte hadn't jeered. She'd tried to stop the parade, had failed, and the three women had walked their walk of shame.

And in Réjane the incident had ignited the flame that would propel her into politics many years later.

Getting the story out of her, though — getting anything connected with the war out of her — was like getting blood from a stone. Well, he now knew why. Some of it at least.

Driving through Orléans was a nightmare. Near Chartres, the gates stayed closed at a railway crossing for what seemed hours. Roadworks on the outskirts of Tours caused yet another delay.

There were only two newspaper people, Yannick saw, standing at the foot of one of the two circular towers that formed the gatehouse, the entrance to the grounds of the d'Aucourte manoir.

It was still early, of course. He pulled to a halt on the grass in front of them, wound down the window and leaned out.

'Anything happening?'

Both men shook their heads.

'What about you?' the older of the two asked. 'You here for anything special?'

Yannick's turn to shake his head. He looked at his watch as he continued on down the drive. Five to nine. Perfect. He'd be finished by ten, ten-thirty. Lucie need never know.

* * *

'That must be it, Dad. Two, three hundred metres further on. Where those two cars are. Turn right.' Apprehension and excitement mixed uneasily in Lucie's voice. 'Hey, isn't that-'

'Yannick's car. It certainly looks like his.' Ray's voice, too, held a question as an all too familiar green car with black soft-top pulled out into the road, heading fast in the opposite direction.

A lump formed in Lucie's throat as she watched it disappear. In the last few weeks they'd travelled all over, sometimes in his car, sometimes in hers.

She sighed. So many happy, shared, memories.

But she didn't understand. What had he been doing here? Another interview with Réjane d'Aucourte? Today?

'Looks like we've got a welcoming party,' her stepfather said as he slowed to turn into the gravelled drive.

With an effort of will, Lucie forced all thoughts of Yannick out of her mind.

Great circular towers rose either side of the entrance, bridging at their first and second storeys to form a massive arched gateway. Two men stood in the shadow thrown by the right-hand tower, watching their arrival.

'Reporters,' Lucie said, seeing the younger one, in his teens still, look at her and scribble something in his notebook while the older man held a camera to his eye.

The drive was long and lined on each side by the neat pompom shapes of pollarded lime trees.

Beyond were lawns, vivid green despite the summer's heat, and further away still, trees growing singly or in groups. There were birds in profusion, and Lucie glimpsed a red squirrel darting across the grass and up a tree.

There was none of the formal elegance of Versailles or Fontainebleau. The wilder, untamed beauty of natural things was master here, and it stole her breath away.

The drive broadened into a turning circle and Ray brought his Rover to a halt under the spreading branches of an unpollarded lime.

Lucie got out of the car slowly, looking up and around her as she did so. It had been over an hour's drive from Tours, and she stretched her stiff legs and smoothed down the skirt of the sky-blue 1940s dress she wore, another jumble sale bargain.

'It's beautiful,' she breathed, easing her hair away from the back of her neck. It was hot already, even though it was only mid-morning. 'The whole place is beautiful. Yannick never said.'

The tuffeau walls of the *manoir* gleamed in the August sunshine. Windows sparkled and the flowers that grew at some of the window ledges provided bright splashes of colour against the creamy white stonework.

Ray checked all the doors of the car were locked before joining her. He put his arm across her shoulders.

'Are you sure you don't want me to go in there with you?'

Lucie looked across at the double flight of steps and the tall doors she would soon be going through, and she swallowed against the dryness in her mouth.

It was a daunting prospect. Who knew what awaited her on the other side?

'I'm scared,' she admitted. 'My mind pictures a scene where I'm like Perdita in 'The Winter's Tale'. You remember, where her mother is overwhelmed with happiness to find the daughter she's never known. But what if it's not like that? What if it's the exact opposite?'

Ray drew her round to face him, placing his hands on her upper arms.

'Lucie, my dear, whatever happens in there, you know you'll always be my daughter. We'll always be your family, me, Arlette . . . ' He stopped.

He'd been about to say 'Yannick', she thought bleakly. She sketched a shaky smile.

'I'd better go.' And it seemed the hardest thing she'd ever done, to pull away from her stepfather and cross the gravel to the steps and those tall, imposing doors.

Worlds Apart

'Réjane?' Eléonore Fournier looked with an uncertain frown from the young woman down below who had just stepped out of a shiny foreign car, to her daughter who stood by her side, and back to the young woman. 'Réjane?'

Réjane couldn't speak. She stroked her mother's arm, linked through hers, and patted her hand. The two women stood close to the window in Eléonore's bedroom and had watched as the car pulled to a halt beneath the lime tree.

It was her hair. She somehow hadn't expected that. Such beautiful hair. Thick, gleaming in the sun, curling untamed. If he had lived in an earlier century and grown his hair long, it would have looked exactly like that.

And her face. She was looking up at the building, and it was like looking into the mirror, at herself as she'd been

212

20 odd years before. No wonder her mother was confused.

And her dress. Where had she found that dress? Knee-length and with square military shoulders and a narrow-cut skirt — a style designed to use as little fabric as possible — it took Réjane straight back to those wartime years. It was like seeing herself as she must have looked to . . .

She gave her mother's hand another pat. 'She's my daughter.'

'But she looks just like you. Not at all like him.'

'Do you think so?' A man in his 40s or 50s had got out of the driver's side and was making his way round to the young woman, had put his arm round her shoulders. Her stepfather, it had to be. He looked a kindly man, and she was glad.

'The colonel.' Eléonore's voice brought her out of her thoughts. 'So handsome in his uniform.'

She sighed and gave her mother's hand a little squeeze.

'She's got his hair,' she said gently,

and there was sadness in her eyes as she added, 'And I rather think she's got his spirit and courage, too.'

She stepped back from the window, bringing her mother with her.

'Come over to the bed now, *mère*. It's time for your rest.'

Just moments later, she smoothed the rug across her mother's lap and blew her a kiss.

'Sweet dreams.'

Leaving Eléonore's bedroom, she walked rapidly along to her husband's room and knocked on his door.

'You were right, Corentin,' she said. 'Or rather, David was. She does look like me.'

Both she and her husband looked straight ahead as they walked along the corridor to the wide staircase which would take them down to the ground floor.

Their guest wouldn't be kept waiting. The maid had been asked to take her to the cloakroom where she could freshen up if she wanted, and then to show her into the salon. Even so, Réjane felt the need to hurry.

Corentin cleared his throat.

'Look, I'll say it again. I'm sorry . . .'

'We'll discuss it after she's gone, shall we?'

Both fell silent. The brisk rap of two sets of soles and heels on the marble flooring echoed the fast erratic beat of Réjane's heart.

What am I going to find? What will she be like? Not physically. I've seen her. I know what she's like to look at. But what will she be like as a person? Will she be like me? Will she have the same tastes as me? Like the same things? Will we share the same values? The same politics? Please God, let her not be a rabid left-winger like my campaign manager. Or a loony right-winger like my opponent.

Or will she be like her adoptive mother, hold her values, share her likes and dislikes? Will she have her mannerisms and twist her hair or pleat her skirt just because her adoptive mother did?

Will I like her? What if I just don't like her?

Will she like me?

She was at the door to the salon. She stood frozen for that instant as Corentin reached past her to turn the handle and push the door open.

★ ★ ★

Lucie sat in one of the two armchairs by the window, leafing through a magazine without seeing a word. She looked up when she heard the door open and her pulses leaped. An elegant woman, long dark hair drawn back into a French pleat. It was her.

There was someone with her, a tall, good-looking man in his 50s. Corentin d'Aucourte, she thought with a pang of disappointment. She'd hoped they'd be alone.

Putting the magazine back on the low table and picking up her shoulder bag, she got to her feet and stepped forward to greet the woman she knew was her mother.

It was strange. In her dreams she'd

pictured herself falling into her mother's arms, and they'd be laughing and hugging and crying for joy.

But the reality was, and the breath caught like dust in her throat, the reality was that she didn't know the woman who stood in front of her.

They were so close, barely a metre separated them, yet a wealth of unshared experience kept them apart.

The Story Unfolds

'Lucie. I'm Réjane.' 'Réjane', and not 'your mother', Lucie noticed. Did she too sense the distance between them? 'This is my husband, Corentin d'Aucourte.'

'It's a pleasure to meet you, mademoiselle.' He took her hand in a brief handshake.

Her mother's hands, with their long slender fingers just like her own, Lucie saw, stayed clasped across her stomach. She was slim and casually elegant in a knee-length dress gently tailored to follow the body's curves without fitting too closely. It was a glimpse, Lucie felt, of herself as she would look when she was in her 40s.

'I have to ask.' Réjane's voice held a hint of apology. 'Just to look at you, I know the truth of it but I have to ask for form's sake. I'd like to know when and where you were born, Lucie.'

'Poitiers, twenty-ninth of July, 1944. I've got the papers here.' That was another strange thing, Lucie thought, drawing an envelope from her bag and holding it out.

Corentin d'Aucourte reached across to take it from her. Her mother was tall, as tall as she was. Yet she'd somehow imagined she would be shorter, the same height as her adoptive mother Margot.

'And the names you were given at birth?'

'Mélusine Jeanne France.'

Réjane looked at her husband who nodded as he folded the documents and put them back in their envelope before returning it to Lucie.

'OK, the inquisition's over.' Réjane smiled a smile of genuine warmth and Lucie couldn't help smiling back. The older woman turned to her husband.

'Corentin, could you leave us, please. I'd like to be alone with Mademoiselle Curtis.'

'Very well.' He touched the knot of his tie, and Lucie sensed displeasure, carefully masked, in his tone. 'I'll be in my office if you need me.'

Neither woman spoke. Lucie heard the door close behind Corentin d'Aucourte, but she hadn't watched him go. Her eyes were fixed on her mother, her mother's on her.

Réjane's head was tilted to one side, and Lucie knew the smile that brought a glow to her mother's features was mirrored in her own face.

Réjane took both Lucie's hands in hers and still neither woman spoke, each absorbed in looking at the other, each deep in her own thoughts.

Now Lucie knew where she got her pale green eyes with their flecks of hazel from, and the strong arc of her eyebrows. Though her hair, despite a superficial resemblance, was lighter and curlier, the shape of her face, with the firm lines of nose and jaw, was the same as her mother's.

She'd read so much about her mother in the last couple of days and had studied so many photos of her in newspapers and magazines, but it hadn't prepared her.

The awkwardness of the first few minutes of their meeting had gone. There was warmth in her mother's look, and Lucie wondered if the barely perceptible change in her had anything to do with her husband's departure.

Réjane squeezed Lucie's hands.

'I can't believe it.' Her voice was husky with emotion. 'You're my child. The daughter I never thought I'd ever see again.'

Lucie couldn't speak. This was the moment when the music should swell and the two of them should fall laughing, hugging, crying into each other's arms. But it wouldn't happen.

Their tie of blood was an intellectual construct, not an emotional one, and there was a sense of reserve, on Lucie's side at least, which prevented any such action.

She found her voice at last.

'I've got so many questions to ask you.'

'As have I, my dearest Lucie.' Réjane let go one of Lucie's hands to bring hers up, fingers curled into the palm, as though to stroke the backs of them along her daughter's cheek. But her hand dropped back down and Lucie thought her mother, too, was conscious of a certain reserve.

'I want to know all about the couple who adopted you. Did you have a happy childhood? Are you happy now?'

Lucie nodded.

'Yes to both questions. I was lucky.'

'Good. I'm glad. Come and sit with me by the window. We've got a lot of catching up to do, haven't we? Tell me about your childhood. Tell me everything you can remember.'

★ ★ ★

Réjane had been wrong to worry. She did like her, and more. Much more.

The sense of wonder Réjane had felt when she first saw her daughter, heard her voice, held her hand had stayed with her. She was blessed with a daughter who was beautiful in both looks and character, who was quick and clever, determined and resourceful. A smile played over her lips, her whole face. Lucie, her little Mélusine, her daughter.

He would have been so proud of her.

They sat near the window, side by side, each armchair turned towards the other so that their knees touched from time to time.

Both women were leaning forward, and Réjane held Lucie's hands between hers. They seemed to have been talking for hours although a glance at her watch told Réjane it had only been one.

It hadn't been easy. She'd heard about the cold, hungry years after Lucie's adoptive father's death, and why she'd changed her name after her arrival in England.

Racked by guilt, Réjane had lowered her eyes, unable to look her daughter in the face when she heard these two stories. She should have been there to ease her daughter's suffering.

But she'd heard too about the happy

times, Lucie's success at school, the friends she'd made and above all, the parents who had loved and supported her through childhood, adolescence and beyond into adulthood.

''You can't keep the child. It's impossible.'' Réjane's mouth twisted. 'My mother's words when she found out I was expecting you — I can hear them now as clearly as if it were yesterday.'

Eléonore's voice had been fierce with fury, she recalled, the memory bringing tears to her eyes.

''No-one must ever know,' my mother said. I was engaged to marry Corentin d'Aucourte. It wasn't a love match, though I did come to love him. He was fourteen years older than me. I hardly knew him. My parents and his had arranged it when I was a child, a business arrangement where both sides profited.'

Her tone was dry, matter-of-fact. She tried to keep it that way. But she was aware that the words came in short, painful bursts, and tears were close to the surface.

'So you used the law the Vichy government had brought in, and gave birth to me anonymously.'

'Yes. I was sent away, to my grandmother's in Poitiers, before I started to show.' Her smile was bleak. 'There was an explosion near the clinic just minutes after you were born. Everyone rushed off to see what was happening. That meant I had you all to myself, in my arms, for half an hour.

'I cut a tiny curl of your hair and wrapped it in a piece of scrap paper. I knew that that, and the memory of your face, the way your little arms and legs moved, would be all I'd have of you when they took you away.'

She fell silent. But there was more. She hadn't finished yet. All at once it was hard to look her daughter in the face.

'I was so happy to hold you, the proudest mother in all the world. And I was sad, deeply unhappy because I knew what was to come. But I was ashamed, too. Even now, I'm ashamed.

Surely I could have been stronger.
Surely I could have insisted on keeping
my precious baby daughter.'

226

Horrific Secret

Lucie's thoughts were swirling. Though her mother's grief was almost too painful to see, she was clearly more than glad to be reunited with the child she'd given away 24 years before. So why had it taken her, Lucie's, phone call to bring mother and daughter together?

She squeezed her mother's hands, stroking the fingers with her thumbs.

'Tell me about my father,' she invited.

She saw her mother draw in a breath, redirecting her thoughts.

'Johann Zimmermann. He was German, a colonel in the army of occupation here in France.'

'Ah.' Ever since she'd found out she was adopted, she'd half-suspected her father was German and had been in the armed forces. It came as no great surprise. 'Was?' she asked quietly.

'He was killed in the fighting some

time towards the end of June 1944.'

'Gestapo?'

A shake of the head.

It was strange, Lucie thought, but she felt no emotional attachment — for the moment, at least — to the man who'd been her father. She could ask questions about him, listen to the replies, in a purely objective, dispassionate way. A thought occurred.

'My middle name, Jeanne, it's — '

'The feminine form of Johann, yes.' Her mother smiled. 'In many ways you look like him, *ma chère*. Your hair, that thick rich hair of yours.' She drew in another long breath before going on.

'During the war, we always had German officers billeted here at the *manoir*. Two, usually, sometimes more. Johann was posted here at the beginning of 1943.

'And I — well, I fell in love with him from the word go. He was good-looking of course, but he was also cultured, interesting. He had all kinds of stories. He was kind, thoughtful of others.

'He was a year older than Corentin but, at the time, I felt I had far more in common with him than I did with my future husband.'

She spoke slowly, softly, and Lucie didn't press her. Her thoughts were clearly far away, in a time and place where she'd been very happy.

'I was young, only seventeen. Part of the attraction for me, at least to start with, was the element of danger in our relationship. If my parents had found out, they wouldn't have approved. No-one would. But very soon, there was more to it than that. Far more. We loved each other deeply. We saw each other as often as we could.

'I told myself I was doing a valuable job for the Resistance, passing on information I learned from the German officers billeted here and those that came to visit.

'But I never passed on anything I learned from Johann. Not that I learned much. He was very conscious of his duty as a soldier. He was an honourable man, fair and just — and tight-lipped when it came to military matters.'

Another long intake of breath.

'I never told them, but I think my parents guessed he was the father of the child I was carrying. They sent me away anyway. Perhaps they sensed the tide of the war was turning against the Germans.

'We wrote, Johann and I. He was overjoyed that he was going to be a father, and he took it for granted we'd get married. Then came the Normandy landings, and shortly afterwards he was moved to the Atlantic coast.'

Her eyes, over-bright, looked inward.

'That was the last time I heard from him. Some weeks later, my father showed me the headline on the front page of the local newspaper here — he'd been killed in the bitter fighting up near Nantes.' Her voice caught, faltered an instant. 'He was gone, and I never even got to say goodbye to him.'

Her mother was silent, and Lucie couldn't speak. Her throat ached as details of her mother's story flashed in and out of her mind. Her mother's love for the man who was her father was palpable, even now, after so many years. But one thing puzzled her.

'His death was the headline? Here?'

'Yes.' Abruptly, Réjane sat back in her chair, her hands slipping away from Lucie's. All at once the expression in her eyes was unreadable. 'When the Allies landed in Normandy, the Germans knew it was the beginning of the end. But they fought on, and any unrest in the population was ruthlessly suppressed.

'There was an incident of sabotage — part of the railway line near here was blown up. The culprits weren't found, so hostages were taken, fifteen of them.'

Lucie's skin crawled. There was a tonelessness in her mother's voice that was frightening to hear.

'Johann — Colonel Zimmermann — was ordered to organise the execution squad.' She hesitated, and tears were spilling down her cheeks. 'Yes, he was following orders, but he still did it, had them shot.

He still murdered those fifteen innocent people.' She stood up, smoothing her skirt down in tight, hard movements, and crossed over to the window, looking out, her back to her daughter.

'No.' The word was no more than a breath. Lucie couldn't take it in. Now, at least, she understood why François Lemercier had spat his anger and disgust.

'Memories are long around here. He's hated — with justification — even today.' Réjane glanced over her shoulder at her daughter.

'So there you have it. I've never spoken about myself and Johann, the relationship we had. When I decided to run for parliament, I thought it had all been buried so long, I'd simply make sure it stayed buried.' She smiled a rueful smile. 'But I hadn't reckoned on you. And that young man of yours.'

'Yannick?' The green car with the black soft-top — it had been his! 'He's not my . . . Why was he here this morning?'

As her mother came towards her, Lucie got to her feet. They stood facing each other, less than a metre apart. Réjane's smile now was full of warmth. She reached out, stroking her daughter's cheek with the tips of her fingers.

'I hope we'll see a great deal of each other from now on, *ma fille*. But for now, go to Yannick. He loves you very much, and I can see from your face you love him too. Ask him what he was doing here this morning.'

'I must go to Yannick, yes.' All at once it was a matter of urgency for Lucie to find him.

'Yes, you must.' Clearly catching a note almost of desperation in her tone, her mother pulled her into a quick, heartfelt hug.

The Look of Love

Moments later Lucie ran down the steps from the manoir and across to her stepfather's car.

'She is my mother. I'm so happy. But we've got to find Yannick.' The words came in breathless gasps.

Ray threw the book he'd been reading on to the back seat.

'We'll see if he's at his mother's,' he said, pushing the car into gear and heading fast down the drive. 'If he isn't, I'll drive you to Paris.'

In Tours, they parked by the Loire. As they turned the corner into the square, Lucie looked up at the second floor of Arlette's house.

And there he was, at the lounge window, looking out.

He caught sight of her at the exact same moment, and his face lit up, she was sure of it, and her pulse leaped wildly.

234

She broke into a run, reaching the main door just as Yannick opened it from the inside.

About to throw herself into his arms, she checked. Something — his expression, the look in his eyes — held her back.

'Let's walk, Lucie. There are things I have to tell you.'

She barely registered the brief, reassuring squeeze Ray gave her arm before going through the main door.

There was a hollow, empty feeling in her stomach. Yannick had been pleased to see her. She knew he had. Why was he now so cool, so distant?

But she knew why. She'd hurt him deeply, questioned his integrity as a journalist. And he probably couldn't forgive her. That was why.

They walked side by side, not touching.

'She is my mother,' Lucie said.

'I know, and I'm very glad for you. I mean that from the bottom of my heart.'

'Thank you.' She blinked back a tear. 'She said I should ask you why you went to see her this morning.'

'Yes. That's what I wanted to talk to you about.'

For a long moment he said nothing more. They walked on. Lucie barely noticed the shops, the people they passed, the direction they were going, and sensed it was the same for Yannick.

She longed to reach out, take his hand in hers, feel him close to her, but something held her back.

'I didn't want to see you hurt,' he said at last. 'I had to know how she was going to receive you. Whether she was going to welcome you with open arms. Or — send you packing.'

Lucie's thoughts flew back to that meeting with her mother, so longed-for, so dreaded.

'It was with open arms,' she said, and there was breathless wonder still in her voice.

'I know I shouldn't have interfered. I shouldn't have gone to see her this

236

morning. Can you forgive me, Lucie?'
His face was anxious.

She stopped in her tracks.

'Forgive you? Oh, Yannick, of course
I forgive you.'

He too had stopped, and he took her
hands in both of his.

'I've said some harsh things.'

Lucie looked into his eyes.

'And I've said some unforgivable
things to you. Whatever you've said or
done, Yannick, you've always had my
best interests at heart.' She smiled.

'My mother's too, I think. I know
that now. I'll never doubt you again.'

'Lucie.' With a sound low in his
throat, he drew her to him, squashing
the breath out of her as he wrapped her
in his arms.

And her heart swooped into a faster
beat as she melted against the lean
strength of his body. It felt right, so
right.

His hands were at her nape, fingers
tangling in her hair, and his lips claimed
hers in a slow, intense kiss.

Long minutes later he lifted his head.

'We can't stay here, Lucie, in the middle of the street,' he said softly, stroking a strand of her hair back from her face. 'Let's walk.'

They walked slowly, arm in arm, heading towards the river. Like two people very much in love, Lucie thought, and there was an ache in her throat.

'What I don't understand . . . ' she started to say, then broke off, changing tack. 'Is David Lucas somehow connected with her?'

Yannick nodded.

'Yes, he's the d'Aucourtes' cellar master, it turns out. He's in charge of wine-making on the estate. I've been to the d'Aucourtes' *manoir* quite a few times, but I never came across him, either before or since that day in Tours.'

'That off-key, so-called interview with me, yes. After meeting me that day, he must have told her who I was. She'd have known I was her daughter.

'So why didn't she get in touch with me? If I hadn't phoned her, three weeks later . . . ' She faltered. If she hadn't phoned — it didn't bear thinking about.

'Lucie, she didn't know about you.'

'But . . .'

'When you phoned her, she realised something was wrong, and managed to piece various parts of the jigsaw together. This morning she told me what actually happened.'

Lucie drew in a shaky breath.

'Go on, Yannick. Please. Tell me everything, from the beginning.'

He was silent for a moment, eyes narrowing, clearly ordering his thoughts.

'It started with the first interview I had with her. She was running for election to parliament, so one of the questions I asked her was if she was squeaky clean. And there was just the tiniest pause before she said yes, she was.'

'And that was enough to tell you she had a secret,' Lucie said. 'You decided to do some sleuthing. I remember you telling me at the time.'

'She'd glanced at the photo on her

desk of herself and her husband, so I began with the family business. There's always plenty of scope for fraud or tax-dodging in the wine industry.

'She found out about me making enquiries. As well as giving me a roasting for invading her privacy, she decided to make her own enquiries to check that her secret was safe.

'Her husband, Corentin d'Aucourte, didn't know about you. She'd never told him, and as the years went by it became more and more difficult to do so.'

'Just like Margot with me and Dad,' Lucie murmured.

'She phoned Poitiers town hall and the woman she spoke to happened to mention a young woman 'born under X' who was trying to find her birth mother. You,' Yannick added with a smile.

'Réjane was certain you weren't her daughter, though,' Yannick continued, 'because she'd been very insistent her daughter should have the names Mélusine Jeanne.

'But just to make sure, she asked David Lucas to meet you.'

'And he knew my names were Mélusine Jeanne France. I told him.'

Yannick shook his head.

'We have to go back to before that meeting with David Lucas. Réjane asked him to meet you, but he refused. And, because he felt his loyalties lay with her husband rather than with her, he told Corentin.'

'Oh!'

'The secret was out. Her husband was furious she'd kept something so important from him but after a few days he calmed down — or seemed to, at least. He was thinking of the succession, he told Réjane, and between them they came up with the idea of David pretending to work for a film company.'

'He interviewed me,' Lucie said, 'found out I was the daughter she'd given birth to before her marriage to Corentin d'Aucourte, and . . .'

'Unknown to Réjane, he reported back to Corentin who wanted the whole affair neatly buried and told him to lie. David then told Réjane your name was Lucie Anne and that you'd been born in 1945.'

'I wasn't her daughter — or so she thought. That's why she saw no reason to contact me.'

'Exactly.'

Lucie didn't speak straight away.

'It worked out all right in the end.' Her voice was husky with emotion. 'She wants to see me again.'

Yannick stopped walking and drew her round into his arms.

'I'm very happy for you, Lucie, my sweet,' he said gently. 'You've got a whole new family now. Two half-brothers and, above all, a mother.'

He reached up, the pad of his thumb tracing a lazy line down her nose and on to her lower lip.

'I won't be writing the story, but if it all comes out, she doesn't mind any more.

'Corentin knows the truth and has accepted it. It might damage her political career, she knows that. But if she's elected, she's decided she'll work to reform the 'born under X' law.'

'Oh, Yannick.'

One day, very soon, Lucie would tell him all she'd learned about her father, knowing Yannick would help her come to terms with both the good and the bad in him.

She looked now into the face of the man she loved. His hands were at her waist, holding her against the warmth of his body. Desire flared deep inside her, fierce and urgent.

'I love you so much.'

'Lucie — I never thought I'd hear those words.' He paused before continuing. 'I'm a journalist. I deal in facts. You told me once I was a realist, and you were right. But you've shown me something very precious, Lucie, sweetheart.

'You've shown me you can have a dream, an impossible dream — and sometimes that dream comes true. I can never thank you enough for showing me that.'

His gaze, full of love, moved from her eyes to her nose to her mouth.

'I've asked you before and I'm asking you again. Will you marry me, Lucie? Will you make me the happiest man alive?'

And she smiled a soft smile as she reached up to run her fingertip slowly along the line of his mouth.

'Yes, Yannick. Yes.'

We do hope that you have enjoyed reading this large print book.

Did you know that all of our titles are available for purchase?

We publish a wide range of high quality large print books including:
Romances, Mysteries, Classics
General Fiction
Non Fiction and Westerns

Special interest titles available in large print are:
The Little Oxford Dictionary
Music Book, Song Book
Hymn Book, Service Book

Also available from us courtesy of Oxford University Press:
Young Readers' Dictionary
(large print edition)
Young Readers' Thesaurus
(large print edition)

For further information or a free brochure, please contact us at:
Ulverscroft Large Print Books Ltd.,
The Green, Bradgate Road, Anstey,
Leicester, LE7 7FU, England.
Tel: (00 44) 0116 236 4325
Fax: (00 44) 0116 234 0205

TWICE IN A LIFETIME

Jo Bartlett

It's been eighteen months since Anna's husband Finn died. Craving space to consider her next steps, she departs the city for the Cornish coast and the isolated Myrtle Cottage. But the best-laid plans often go awry, and when Anna's beloved dog Albie leads her away from solitude and into the path of Elliott, the owner of the nearby adventure centre, their lives become intertwined. As Anna's attraction to Elliott grows, so does her guilt at betraying Finn, until she remembers his favourite piece of advice: you only live once . . .

WILD SPIRIT

Dawn Knox

It's Rae's dream to sail away across oceans on her family's boat, the *Wild Spirit* — but in 1939 the world is once again plunged into conflict, and her travel plans must be postponed. When Hitler's forces trap the Allies on the beaches of Dunkirk, Rae sails with a fleet of volunteer ships to attempt the impossible and rescue the desperate servicemen. However, her bravery places more lives than her own in jeopardy — including that of Jamie MacKenzie, the man she's known and loved for years . . .

RETURN TO TASMANIA

Alan C. Williams

Heading back from Sydney to her idyllic childhood home in Tasmania, Sandie's priorities are to recover from a bullet wound, reconsider her future in the police, and spend time with her sister and niece. But even as the plane lands, she senses that a fellow passenger is not all he seems. When a series of suspicious events follow her arrival, the mystery man reveals himself as Adam, who has been sent to protect Sandie's family as they become embroiled in the fall-out following the double-crossing of a dangerous criminal.

THE ENGLISH AU PAIR

Chrissie Loveday

Stella Lazenby flies to Spain to work as an au pair for Isabel and Ignacio Mendoza, looking after their sons Juan and Javier. The parents are charming, the boys delightful — and then there's the handsome Stefano, who becomes more than a friend . . . But all is not as perfect as it seems. Housekeeper Maria resents Stella's presence, and Isabel worries that her husband is hiding secrets. Then Stefano is accused of stealing from Ignacio's company, and Stella doesn't know what to believe . . .

DANGER FOR DAISY

Francesca Capaldi

Mature student Daisy Morgan plucks up her courage to attend a get-together — only to cannon straight into a handsome gentleman, spilling her drink all over his smart suit into the bargain! To make matters worse, he turns out to be Seth, her flatmates' archaeologist friend. After this unconventional meeting, sparks quickly kindle between the pair, and Daisy accompanies Seth to a dig on a remote island. But danger lurks on Sealfarne — and they are about to unearth it . . .